倍斯特出版事業有限公司
Best Publishing Ltd.

新托福10

iBT

寫作

QRCODE
DOWNLOAD

韋爾
倍斯特編輯部
◎合著

《三大學習特色》

口、筆譯單句練習 提升對各種句型的掌握能力和臨場反應力

外文暢銷書內容加持 有效鞏固陳述的論點可信度、強化說服力

「獨立篇」：從範文提升對複雜句型的掌握，寫出用語恰當、準確且流暢的文句，
　　　　　並運用外文暢銷書觀點充分闡述論點脫穎而出，一次就考取高分。

「整合篇」：強化「聽」講座能力，比對聽力講座和閱讀內容的相似或差異處，
　　　　　有效針對話題完成任務，輕易戰勝整合題作文。

Editor's preface

作者序

　　新托福的口說或寫作題庫中，許多考題都與我們生活息息相關，但是某些時候我們卻很難構思出嚴謹的論述、提出獨特的見解、表達具體且不鬧出笑話的文句。尤其在寫作中，適時展現自己對複雜語句的掌握度確實能大幅提升所獲取的成績。（前提是你的文法修辭都要沒有問題。）但是更重要的一點是，你要知道自己在表達什麼，考生常寫出許多不具體且缺乏理據的論述。

　　這樣說可能很空泛（這樣的話僅是造了文法正確但卻 general 的 statements），所以我們從例子來看好了。例如在學歷相關的議題好了，學歷到底是否重要呢？有考生寫了「既然比爾・蓋茲或臉書創辦人都輟學去創業了，所以學歷不重要」，很多時候考生造了類似這樣的句子，僅僅寫出了文法正確的句子但卻是未能充分解釋該寫作題題目問的問題。而且當中還牽涉到這個論點是正確的嗎？還有論述的合理性等很多問題。

在 The Third Door 中，作者也面臨了這樣的問題，作者在追尋夢想和學業中需要作出選擇，他向自己的好友兼 mentor（Elliott）說道，他想向父母提他要輟學的事。（因為他想到成功人士像是比爾・蓋茲和馬克・佐克伯也是從學校輟學後創業，而且他們後來也很成功，像極了在口說或寫作中許多考生會作出的一些相關論述，但這些論述是缺乏查證和不具說服力。）

面對他的問題，Elliott 並未給予作者直接的答案，只對作者說道"Bill Gates and Mark Zuckerberg didn't drop out the way you think they did. Do some research."。在查完資料後，作者發現自己很無知，像是 Zuckerberg 被 venture capitalist 問到是否要 drop out of the school，Zuckerberg 回答說「他計畫要繼續他大三的課業」，最後對於臉書前景有更好的實務方法時，也只說了"take a semester off"，而非"drop out of school"。在 Bill Gates 方面則是"Gates didn't impulsively drop out of college either. He took just one semester off during junior year to work full-time on Microsoft."。書中所傳達的這些訊息，除了導正我們的思考外，也能讓我們在新托福口說和寫作中寫出合乎理據的論點，讓考官可以清楚知道你對這個議題是否具有批判性思考且將議題的論點充分闡釋出。

書中的獨立篇作文就是以這樣的精神為基礎，當中融入了許多暢銷書或書籍作為輔助，能有效協助考生寫出具說服力的語句並一舉獲取高分，免於造出許多 too general 但僅是文法正確的語句，而卡在某個分數段上，苦思到底問題在哪裡。在整合篇的部分，書中則選取了考生較不熟悉的話題，像是美國文學和哲學的部分，考生可以藉由這些議題強化自己對該主題的熟悉度，在新托福寫作中拿到理想成績。

韋爾 敬上

新托福寫作包含了兩種形式的測驗模式即「**獨立題型**」和「**整合題型**」。獨立題型是傳統的看完一個題目段落後，撰寫一篇約 300 字左右的英文作文，而整合篇則涉及了**閱讀**、**聽力**和**寫作**三項技能，考生會需要先閱讀一小段文章，緊接著聽一段講座，最後根據聽力和閱讀的內容撰寫一篇文章。後者對於考生來說可能比較需要時間去適應。整合題的關鍵點在於聽力部分，所以也可以多加強記筆記。

　　在獨立題型中，作者在回答內容中加入了暢銷書籍等，能夠大幅提升考生湊字數、改善語句 redundant 等的問題。考生在某些時候因為不知道要寫什麼了或無形中又寫了好幾句其實跟上句內容重複或相似的概念，又或者是論點太 general 且無說服力，這些都會影響考生考到一定分數的寫作成績。此外，書籍中在獨立篇加入了單句筆譯（中譯英），在整合篇加入了口譯（中譯英），這些都能協助考生掌握更複雜的句式、文句表達更多樣、聽懂聽力、口說和寫作測驗中的講座內容，以及強化口語測驗中的表達能力。最後祝考生都能獲取理想成績。

倍斯特編輯部 敬上

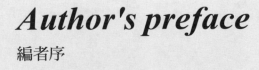

Author's preface
編者序

Today's young people are like roses in a greenhouse, compared with young people in the past. Young people can do nothing about it simply because they have accustomed to what their parents will do for them right after they come out of mother's womb. It has become a habit that their parents will do things as trivial as cleaning to something as major as writing a resume and making a phone call to the company's HR personnel. Some parents even go to the interview with their kids and doing all the talking. All these make interviewers not convince candidates' ability to do the job. From all these reasons, perhaps today's parents should dial back to how parents raised kids from the previous generations so that kids can develop a sound mindset and decision-making ability. Therefore, I think these statements are so true.

現今的年輕人就像是溫室的玫瑰般，跟過去年輕人相比的話。年輕人卻束手無策因為他們已經適應了從母親子宮出生後，父母都會替他們打算的日子了。這已經成了習慣，父母們會做像是替他們打掃這樣子微不足道的小事至到替他們撰寫履歷和打電話給公司的人事專員，有些父母甚至陪同小孩去參加面試，而且全程都替小孩子回答，這些都讓面試官們無法信服候選人有做這份工作的能力，從這些原因來看，或許今日的父母應該要將事情撥回正軌，撥回至上一代父母如何養育小孩，這樣他們的小孩才能夠發展出健全的心態且具備做決定的能力。因此，我認為這些陳述是很真實的。

Another thing parents should be worried about is online games. Kids can become so addicted to the game that their personality becomes so eccentric. Some even use parents' credit cards to buy weapons in the virtual world because kids want their characters to be more powerful. Others have aggressive behaviors toward friends who play better than they.

另一件事父母需要擔心的是線上遊戲。小孩會變得沉迷遊戲，以至於他們的個性變得相當古怪。有些小孩甚至使用母親的信用卡去購買虛擬世界的武器因為小孩想要讓他們的遊戲角色更強大，其他人對於遊戲中玩得比他們好的朋友有著侵略性的行為。

All these modern-day phenomena make parents tiresome. Kids are like viruses, constantly evolving into a new form, and parents are too tired to combat. One kid even went to the extreme, destroying all furniture at home simply because their parents will not let him buy the new iPhone. His iPhone is not even a half year old. Today's kids' value is aggravated by iPhones and lots of expensive stuff and they do not cherish things. They do not know money is not easily earned.

所有這些現代的現象都使得父母感到疲憊。小孩就像是病毒般，不斷地演化出新的形式，而父母則過於疲憊而無法應付。有位小孩甚至表現得極端，毀壞家裡的所有傢俱僅因為他的父母不讓他購買新的iPhone。他的iPhone甚至才使用不到半年。現今的小孩的價值觀受到iPhone和許多昂貴的物品的影響而加劇崩壞，而且他們不會珍惜

190

「**誇飾**」和「**妙語連珠句**」錦上添花
考官給大心，分數自然就高

- All these modern-day phenomena make parents tiresome. Kids are like viruses, constantly evolving into a new form, and parents are too tired to combat.

- Today's young people are like roses in a greenhouse, compared with young people in the past. Young people can do nothing about it simply because they have accustomed to what their parents will do for them right after they come out of mother's womb. It has become a habit that their parents will do things as trivial as cleaning to something as major as writing a resume and making a phone call to the company's HR personnel.

暢銷書加持 ①
《The Promise of A Pencil: How ordinary Person Can Create Extraordinary Change》

- 使用作者亞當・博朗成長時期父母的教育模式輕鬆迎戰「父母是否該給予小孩等值的物質獎勵題」，從中學習作者父母如何教育出伯朗高材生，並以該實例充分闡述該議題。

🎓 整合能力強化❸ 段落拓展

Sometimes parents reward kids with a great deal of money or other material things, if kids perform well in their exams or win medals in a national or international contest. Do you think parents should use things, such money and material things as incentives to motivate kids to learn?

Step 1 先選定立場，是支持著個論點還是反對呢？
（範文是反對，認為這不是個好的想法）

Step 2 選擇好立場後，構思出核心句型或段落，如範文中的第一個小段落，提到 should be discouraged 和 it is something that should be developed internally，接下來的段落就能由學習應該是由內部化的發展所接續完成。

Step 3 構思出核心句型或第一段落的鋪陳敘述後，第二個段落可以搭配有看過的書籍或名人提過的論點，強化表達跟說服力。更能避免只是寫出文法正確跟句式多樣的句子，但還是讓考官不知所以然，覺得太 general，論點未詳細闡述到。

30

🎓 整合能力強化❸ 段落拓展

Decision making is quite essential in our lives, but nowadays parents tend to be the ones who are responsible for kids' inability to make major decisions and be independent. People from the previous generation; however, had no trouble making a major decision. What do you think about these statements?

Step 1 看完題目後先寫出概述句，定義出「在校園環境是衡量學生伸否有能力自力和能夠對於他們自己本身生活做出重大決定的指標之一。」，這段於後面要寫出題目中提到的「孩子更難獨立跟做決定等」是相關聯的，也更好去延伸段落。

Step 2 選擇好立場後，列出陳述句後緊接著表明事情並非如此，並使用《你如何衡量你的人生》一書中所描述的足球父母們，強化不同意的立場，過度替小孩安排事情的足球父母，造成了小孩子過於依賴等問題，除了呼應首句，也為下個段落作了鋪陳。

Step 3 舉出實例，包含校長和教授接到電話的部分，還有使用詞飾「年輕人替自己做決定的能力不是稍微退步些，而是有

66

暢銷書加持 ②
《How Will You Measure Your Life》

- 運用書中提到的「足球父母（soccer parents）」，在首段切入主題，並反襯出現今父母是如何教育小孩的，再以新聞實例接續論述現今父母的教育方式。

Instructions 使│用│說│明

暢銷書加持 ③
《How Luck Happens》

- 在交友和社交類話題時，利用「弱連結（weak tie）」為重點，從中舉實例講述交新朋友的益處，最後以暢銷書文句再次強化論點，說明交新朋友如何增進一個人的幸運程度並創造出工作和感情雙贏新局面。

🖊 整合能力強化❸ 段落拓展

In our life, we all expect our friendship with other people will remain, but sometimes things do not go as we expected. Some people adopt a more leisure approach by not thinking about the friendship; and therefore, are more likely to retain their friendship with others. Others are fixed on maintaining friendship with a certain cult, thinking that only by doing this can a friendship last and blossom. What is your opinion?

Step 1 題目中有提到對於友誼的兩種看法，先選定其中一個立場或可以像範文這樣先定義友誼，再逐步導入正題，範文指出長時間的維持一段友誼是具有報酬性的，但也會一個人造成某些程度的傷害。

Step 2 次個段落解釋會造成的負面影響。

Step 3 再來，解釋一直交新朋友的益處，例如不會有太大的壓力和比較心態等等的，並說明如此一來你可以更享受與朋友相處的時刻。

Step 4 最後提到另一件關於交新朋友的好處：你總能從不同類型

102

🖊 整合能力強化❸ 段落拓展

Traditional viewpoints have often favored students majoring in engineering and hard science over students of the humanities and social sciences, thinking that the latter has a less promising future right after students graduate from universities. Thus, people are suggesting that we should not major in History or Philosophy. What is your opinion?

Step 1 先思考主修人文社會科學和理工科系的優缺點。主修人文社會科學像是歷史和哲學真的是錯誤的選擇嗎？

Step 2 範文首句提供了很好的定義：
※ 儘管關於選系的傳統觀點有些有事實理據，職涯軌跡並不是能預測的。
※ 人們無法很確定的表明主修某個特定的科系就意謂著你一定會比主修其他科系更成功。
※ 因此我想使用歷史作為例子，講述主修人文和社會科學也能給予你特定的優勢。

（三句話很系統且邏輯性的引入主題。）

114

暢銷書加持 ④
《Getting There》

- 以女CEO史黛西・史奈德為例子，講述人文科系的優勢，她最終修習俄羅斯歷史。修俄羅斯歷史不僅使她更了解自己，也替她未來的成功鋪路，以實例**反駁**修習哲學或歷史對於求職沒有任何助益。

- 工作類話題中剖析具熱情的工作和長工時等的關聯性，並加入暢銷書中「**找到人生至喜（bliss）**」和「**目標應該要放在別人實際上願意付你薪水做你所感到熱情的職業**」的陳述，進一步推論出「當你正在從事你感到熱情的事而且對於別人願意付你薪水做這份工作時，較長的工作時間似乎就不是個麻煩事或困境」。

整合能力強化❸ 段落拓展

Some people say to accumulate wealth in shortest time, one should get a higher salary, but often a high-paid job requires you to spend much longer hours in the office. Others would rather settle down a job that requires less responsibility and workload so that they can have enough rest after a long day at work. What is your opinion?

Step 1 題目中提到兩個相對的看法，各有利弊。可以從自己的工作經驗中回推，這樣會更好發揮這個題目。範文中則是選擇工時較長薪資較高的工作，手段還提到這是「在最短的時間內累積財富是能夠提早退休的方法之一」，選定了其中一個立場。

Step 2 次個段落提到了解自己的重要性，從事工作和長工時都不是重點，因為若是從事自己喜愛的工作就不會有這些顧慮。

Step 3 下個段落提到，自己明確知道自己的目標，並舉例出「不是非常了解自己的人在辦公室工作時會感到痛苦」，更何況工時若加長。並續還「這是因為他們尚未找到自己的熱情和他們在生命中想做的事。」

138

- 使用暢銷書《你如何衡量你的人生》中的兩個具體的舉例講述安排過多的活動對小孩造成的影響，除了引人反思外，也替接續幾個段落預留了伏筆。

整合能力強化❸ 段落拓展

Today's parents arrange an endless array of activities for their kids, leaving them no room to have enough time to rest and truly engage in something they are passionate about. Kids do need time to absorb those things and learning should not be forced and arranged. It should be based on children's interest. What is your opinion?

Step 1 這題是關於子女教育的問題，題目中的敘述呈現了某一個論點，並詢問考生看法為何？若想表達的論點跟題目相同，可以延續繼目中提到的論點並繼續表達看法。如果有其他不同於題目敘述的想法，可以思考一下替小孩安排許多活動更多的優點等。

Step 2 首段除了先定義出「活動和這些意圖對小孩的影響」，接著使用暢銷書「你如何衡量你的人生」中的兩個具體舉例：
※「父母，通常有著心之所向，將自己本身的希望和夢想投射在自己的小孩上面」。

※「當這些其他意圖不知不覺的開始作用時，父母似乎將他們的小孩導向無止盡的活動列表上，但這部非小孩子

150

整合能力強化 ❸ 段落拓展

"Experienced" is a too powerful word used by modern people. Most people are led to believed that experienced professionals, such as doctors and attorneys, perform relatively well than young professionals because they have more experience. What's your opinion?

Step 1 這題提到經驗會有傳統的刻板印象，以至於大家會認為其專業經驗者比年輕的專業人士表現得更好。

Step 2 這題變醫師發揮的，而段落首句先以錘鍊的部分講述並反問真的是如此嗎，接著以其中一個行業，醫生的部分為例去討論。

Step 3 提到大家對於大醫院和小醫院的錯誤認知，並指出這些「誤解選擇在人們心中，而且誤解很難從人們心中剌除。」，最後給拉回這個主題。

Step 4 使用暢銷書「刻意練習：來自新科學專業」具體解釋
※「評論中的幾乎每六十個研究中，醫生的表現隨著時間而呈現更糟的情況或維持不變。」
※「年資較深的醫生所知道的較少而且在提供適當照護

162

暢銷書加持 ⑦

《Peak, Secrets from the New Science of Expertise》

● 運用書籍《刻意練習》的研究數據和給力論述補足一般性論述或坊間佳句，仍無法闡述像是「資深醫生與年輕醫生何者表現較優」等棘手議題，應試時腦筋不再空白或感到不知所措。

影集或電影
搭配《慾望師奶》猛提升「教育類話題」答題能力

● 麗奈特・思嘉夫在第一季時有四個小孩。有次她對著警察宣洩著自己的情緒「**我有四個年紀六歲以下的小孩要養育。我當然會有情緒控管問題**」。

● 麗奈特・思嘉夫花費時間與小孩們從事運動活動，即使她丈夫表明小孩不是打棒球的料，所以他不需要練棒球。但是她想要自己的小孩能夠有著不放棄做任何事的個性。藉由與她的小孩玩棒球，她展現出她的耐心，即使她笑著說：「**如果我把棒球在丟慢些，那就是在打保齡球了**」。

何與兄弟姊妹、朋友、家庭成員合作或是小孩是個良好的團隊合作者嗎？或是小孩是如何解開難題的呢？所有這些事情都是父母在從事學校作業時較輕鬆也要緊的，這比起小孩在數學表現多好或是小孩在拼字比賽上表現多好更重要。這是形塑他們角色和個性的時候，這也是父母和小孩們建議情感連結的時候。

In one of the successful sitcoms, *Desperate Housewives*, it uncovers some wisdom of how parents raise kids or how four housewives raise kids. It is something the audience can learn from. One of the housewives, Lynette Scavo has four kids in season one. One time she vented her emotions to the policeman that "I have four kids under the age of six. I absolutely have anger management issues", but she also demonstrates something related to the topic. She does spend time with her kids by playing sports even if her husband says their kid is not the baseball material so he doesn't have to play.

在一部成功的影集之一《慾望師奶》中，它揭露了一些父母如何養育小孩或是四個主婦如何養育小孩的智慧，這是一些觀眾們能夠學習的部分，其中之一的主婦，麗奈特・思嘉夫在第一季時有四個小孩，有次她對著警察宣洩著自己的情緒「我有四個年紀六歲以下的小孩要養育，我當然會有情緒控管問題。」，但是她卻也展示出一些與這主題相關的部分。她花費時間開與小孩們從事運動活動，即使她丈夫表明他們小孩不是打棒球的料，所以他不需要練棒球。

58

整合能力強化❸ 段落拓展

Job satisfaction is extremely important in the workplace. Some people deem certain types of work, such as clerical work as something repetitive, and they find that work mundane and boring. They would prefer to do something adventurous and challenging. Doing different types of projects in a single workday gives them energy and a sense of fulfillment. What do you think about this? Use specific reasons and examples to support your answer.

Step 1 進一步探討原因，提出對於題目論述的論點。
（題目中提到了兩種類型的工作：工作內容是重複性高的工作和具冒險性和挑戰性的工作；每個人對於工作的偏好不同，範文中提出了令人省思的問題，並進一步探討影響「工作滿意度」的因素，對於話題目有更好掌握度和 facts 的考生，可以選擇像範文中的敘述句做開展）。

Step 2 先寫出鋪陳的句子後，列出了三個主要原因：一個人的個性、產業的類型或是工作內容的熟練度都影響著工作滿意度，接著概述講述著為何同個條件下，工作滿意度會是因人而異，還有提到了工作的重複性。（這三個因素是相互影響的，其實可以探討的部分太廣，可能一篇托福文章也寫

42

段落拓展
工作滿意度話題

看完題目敘述後（不該腦海想到什麼就寫了什麼），先構思出影響工作滿意度的背後因素可能有哪些，例如：① **一個人的個性**、② **產業的類型**或是③ **工作內容的熟練度**都影響著工作滿意度。

- 當構思出主核心後，就能迅速以這三個點切入並寫出數個段落內容，像是「同個條件下，工作滿意度會是因人而異，有些人會喜歡重複性高的工作內容，因為不太需要思考…但是某些個性的人卻會因為工作內容重複性太高，而感到不具挑戰性，因此對於工作滿意度不高…」。

- 另外，如具工作經驗或實習經驗，就更能從工作經驗中回想，進而迅速寫出文章內容…。

中譯英練習

- 從書中獨立篇各單元的中譯英練習迅速累積各種句型，漸進式累積實力到一次下筆就至少寫出300字以上佳句，一次就考到高分。

整合能力強化❷ 單句中譯英演練

在掌握文法句型後，學習者大多能拿到 25 分左右的寫作成績，英語句型多樣性和各式句型是獲取 25 高分的關鍵，現在請演練接下來的單句中譯英練習，請務必演練後再觀看所寫答案，並於觀看答案後仔細貼近語彙，加凡對句與句間之關聯。

❶ 在工作場所中的滿意度是非常難衡量和評估的，這真的因人而異。有時候這關係到一個人的個性、產業的類型或是工作內容的熟練度。

【參考答案】
Satisfaction in the workplace is very hard to measure and evaluate, and it really varies from person to person. Sometimes it is related to the personality of the worker, the type of industry, or dexterity of the job content.

❷ 一方面，不同類型的任務可能給予一個人足夠的空間，能在一項任務和下項任務中轉換而不感到無趣，但是這有時候可能會使腦部承受不住製造或許多憂慮和壓力。

【參考答案】
On the one hand, different types of tasks may give a person enough room to shift from doing one task to another without

38

Instructions 使｜用｜說｜明

整合篇練習 ①

這部分是考生較不熟悉的考試方式，比獨立篇多了聽力和閱讀的部分，所以請務必確實練習這個部分，盡快熟悉這類型的答題，在考試中更能從容應答。

美國文學、
藝術和教育類話題

- 降低因對主題不熟悉而造成的考試失常或失分，**強化美國文學、藝術和教育類**話題演練，立即提升應試答題穩定性，一次就考到理想成績。

高分範文搶先看 ▶ MP3 048

The reading and lecture delineate the contrary styles of utopian and dystopian literature by depicting the representative works and various traits of both literary genres.

閱讀篇章及課堂講述藉由描寫烏托邦及反烏托邦兩種文學類型的代表作品和其特色，勾勒出兩種相反的風格。

First, the reading and the lecture explain the opposite definitions of these two words. Whereas utopia is a deliberately invented word with its origins in Greek, meaning an ideal place or a place that doesn't exist, a dystopia is an atrocious place contrary to a utopia.

首先，閱讀篇章及課堂講述解釋這兩個字的相反定義。烏托邦是一個刻意被創造出的字，源自希臘文，意為理想的地方或不存在之地，相反地，反烏托邦是個險惡之地。

Next, the reading traces back to the earliest utopian fiction, Plato's The Republic , and gives the utopian examples from British literature, which are Jonathan Swift's Gulliver's Travels and Samuel Butler's Erewhon , while the lecture points out that the boundary between utopian and dystopian literature is sometimes not so definite, as both styles are present in the latter two works of fiction.

其次，閱讀篇章追溯至最初的烏托邦小說，柏拉圖的《共和國》，

280

整合篇練習 ②

● 熟悉訊息整合的部分後，請觀看高分範文的部分，此部分能協助考生迅速累積各類句型的「換句話説」能力，使用與「**閱讀文章**」和「**聽力講座**」不重疊的句式表達，再將所有訊息內化後，摘要出關鍵重點，立即獲取高分。

整合能力強化❷ 聽力與口譯表達強化

❶ 貝聿銘從在上海就讀高中快畢業時，他決定到美國念大學。他曾承認這個決定是受到賓·克洛斯比的電影影響，在那些電影裡，美國的大學生活似乎是充滿了歡樂。

_____

ANS:
As Pei's secondary education in Shanghai drew near an end, he decided to enter an American university, a decision which he once admitted was made under the influence of Bing Crosby movies, in which college life in America seemed full of fun.

❷ 雖然他很快就發現嚴格的學術生活和電影的描繪相差甚多，他就讀於麻省理工學院建築系時表現得非常優秀。

_____

ANS:
Though he soon found out that the rigorous academic life differed drastically from the portrayal in movies, he excelled in the architecture school of the Massachusetts Institute of Technology (MIT).

❸ 他尤其被現代建築吸引，現代建築的特色是極簡風和運用玻璃及鋼鐵素材，也是被法蘭克·洛伊·萊特影響。

308

中譯英口譯練習

● 獨家規劃中譯英的口譯練習，可以跟同學兩兩一組練習，同步強化「**口說**」和「**口譯**」能力。

Part 1 獨立篇

CONTENTS

kids. Some prefer to spend most of the time taking their kids traveling, exercising in the park, or visiting museums so that their children can develop their own interests along the way. Others are inclined to set a strict rule for their own kids, learning things solely related to school tests or the college entrance exam. What is your opinion on this topic?

※題目：Decision making is quite essential in our lives, but nowadays parents tend to be the ones who are responsible for kids' inability to make major decisions and be independent. People from the previous generation; however, had no trouble making a major decision. What do you think about these statements?

※題目：Some people proclaim that actions of young people are easily influenced by celebrities, and it is not a good thing. Others think the influence of celebrities on young people can be quite positive and inspiring. What is your opinion?

majoring in engineering and hard science over students of the humanities and social sciences, thinking that the latter has a less promising future right after students graduate from universities. Thus, people are suggesting that we should not major in History or Philosophy. What is your opinion?

※題目：In some books, it reveals an astonishing fact that the average American spends about 9 years in their lifetime watching meaningless TVs or movies. Although it sheds some light for most of us, and watching TVs and movies does have some negative effects on our health, do viewing those have a positive influence on people? What is your opinion?

※題目：Some people say to accumulate wealth in shortest time, one should get a higher salary, but often a high-paid job requires you to spend much longer hours in the office. Others

would rather settle down a job that requires less responsibility and workload so that they can have enough rest after a long day at work. What is your opinion?

※題目：Today's parents arrange an endless array of activities for their kids, leaving them no room to have enough time to rest and truly engage in something they are passionate about. Kids do need time to absorb those things and learning should not be forced and arranged. It should be based on children's interest. What is your opinion?

※題目："Experienced" is a too powerful word used by modern people. Most people are led to believed that experienced professionals, such as doctors and attorneys, perform relatively well than young professionals because they have more experience. What's your opinion?

※題目：People in some nations are eating or used to eat pets, such as dogs and cats, but nowadays people's attitude toward pets have changed. People now adore their pets and are even willing to spend a great deal of money on their them. Some people think this kind of behavior is a bit too much because they are just pets, not children. What is your opinion?

※題目：Today's kids are having more distractions in life. Distractions, such as smartphones, are one of the main reasons that they underperform in the school setting. Some people claim that those distractions are making raising kids so hard nowadays because they even bring the safety issue of their kids to the table, and this is something much more important than getting a good grade. What is your opinion?

Part 2 整合篇

CONTENTS

Part 1 獨立篇

　　獨立篇為一個特定主題，主要是要檢測出考生能否對於一主題提出特別的見解。書籍規劃中加入了暢銷書佳句等，能有效強化論點說服力，跟減低 redundant 句子或 too general 的段落，但能無法清楚闡述一主題的窘境。

　　此外，書籍中規劃了中譯英的練習，可以在練習完作文後，演練中譯英，掌握更多樣的句型表達後再觀看範文答案。範文答案均有錄音，學習效果倍增，快來練習吧！

UNIT 01

教育類話題①：
父母該使用物質來
獎勵或激勵孩童嗎？

 TASK 2 Independent Writing

Directions

Read the question below. You have 30 minutes to plan, write, and revise your essay. Typically, an effective response will contain a minimum of 300 words.

TOPIC

Sometimes parents reward kids with a great deal of money or other material things, if kids perform well in their exams or win medals in a national or international contest. Do you think parents should use things, such money and material things as incentives to motivate kids to learn?

整合能力強化① 實際演練 ▶ *MP3 001*

請自己動手演練並於 30 分鐘內完成至少 300 字的英文文章，盡量以打字的方式進行，因為新托福測驗是電腦考試。

_____

_____

_____

_____

_____

_____

_____

_____

_____

_____

_____

_____

_____

_____

整合能力強化② 單句中譯英演練

在掌握文法句型後，學習者大多能拿到 25 分左右的寫作成績，英語句型多樣性和各式句型是獲取 25⁺高分的關鍵，現在請演練接下來的單句中譯英練習。請務必演練後再觀看答案，並於觀看答案後仔細聆聽音檔，強化對各句型的記憶。

① 使用其他誘因例如，金錢、玩具或是智慧型手機，來激勵小孩學習事物的念頭是該打消的，因為學習應該是經由內部化的發展而成的。

_____

_____

【參考答案】
The use of other incentives, such as money, toys, or smartphones, to motivate kids to learn things should be discouraged because it is something that should be developed internally.

② 只有本能的驅策所導向的學習會持久且最終成為一項習慣，學習者也能終生受益。

_____

_____

【參考答案】
Only an instinctive drive to learn will last long and eventually become a habit that will benefit a person throughout his or her life.

③ 在描述他的童年時期時，作者亞當‧博朗，也有著如同我們大多數的人在青少年時期中存有的疑問，我們是否應該拿到金錢獎勵，如果我們得到高的分數，或是拿到全 A 的成績。

_____

_____

【參考答案】

In describing his childhood, the author Adam Braun had the question, like many of us during our teen days, should we be given money if we get high grades or straight As.

④ 他要求金錢作為他拿到高分的獎勵被他的父親所拒絕，因為他父親堅持不給予小孩金錢的獎勵，或是不以其他誘因來寵壞自己的小孩。

_____

_____

【參考答案】

His request for money as compensation for his high grades was shut down by his father, who stays firm on not giving kids money in return or not indulging their kids with other incentives.

⑤ 對小孩來說，這太模糊了而且小孩們通常會將這個回應理解成「不，我們沒有得到任何相對應的回報」或是「我們的父親只是想不出更好的理由來說服我們」。

_____

_____

27

To kids, it is simply too vague and kids would probably see the response as "No, we are not getting anything in return" or "our father just couldn't think a better excuse to persuade us".

⑥ 在心底，他的父親想要他們抱持著更高的標準，這樣一來他們就能發展出自動自發的本能去學習。

_____

_____

Deep down, his father wants them to hold a higher standard so that they will develop an inherent drive to learn things.

⑦ 或許他的父親應該要向他們的孩子解釋事情脈絡或是或許解釋並不能使得該年紀的孩子們全然理解父親用意的潛在意圖。

_____

_____

Perhaps his father should explain things to their kids or perhaps explanations cannot make kids at that time to fully grasp the underlying meanings.

⑧ 在生命中，我們應該要發展出內在驅策學習事物的能力，這樣我們才能在我們生命艱苦時候，持續生存下去，即使我們不在學校環境了。

_____

【參考答案】

In life, we should develop an inherent drive to learn things so that we can continually survive through the hard times of our life even after we are not in school anymore.

⑨ 仰賴誘因學習事物的人，如果在沒有任何誘因存在時會遭遇巨大的挫折，而且大多數的人沒有辦法在步入職場後有良好的表現，因為有時候職場中不會有誘因來驅策你。

【參考答案】

People relying on incentives to learn things will encounter a huge setback if there are no incentives, and most people cannot perform well when they enter the job market simply because sometimes there are no incentives.

⑩ 只有讓小孩發展出高的標準且有本能驅策學習的能力，才能讓孩子們在他們人生的每個階段都能茁壯成長，即使當下沒有父母的指導或支持。

【參考答案】

Only by letting kids develop a high standard and an inherent drive to learn can they thrive in every phase of their lives, even if there are no parental guidance or parental support.

Sometimes parents reward kids with a great deal of money or other material things, if kids perform well in their exams or win medals in a national or international contest. Do you think parents should use things, such money and material things as incentives to motivate kids to learn?

Step 1 先選定立場，是支持著個論點還是反對呢?
（範文是反對，認為這不是個好的想法）

Step 2 選擇好立場後，**構思出核心句型或段落**，如範文中的第一個小段落，提到 should be discouraged 和 it is something that should be developed internally，接下來的段落學習由內部化發展的論述接續完成。

Step 3 構思出核心句型或第一段落的鋪陳敘述後，第二個段落可以搭配看過的書籍或名人提過的論點，強化表達跟說服力。避免只有寫出文法正確跟句式多樣的句子，論點也未詳細闡述到，這會讓考官不知所以然，覺得太 general。

※ 這篇範文搭配了暢銷書《一支鉛筆的承諾：一位普通人

如何能創造出驚人的改變》。

Step 4　有了暢銷書加持後，就要利用當中的論點協助表達出接續的文句，文中提到了困惑處和他父親堅持不給予小孩金錢的等值獎勵，此能大幅強化我們不支持提供獎勵的論點（可以邊寫邊笑了，因為這又是 28⁺高分了）。

Step 5　有了神助，這個段落要構思出原因，接續寫該父親不支持的原因並接續探討背後隱含的意義。

Step 6　最後拉回所探討的話題並且總結出這是培育小孩子養成內在驅策學習力，而且小孩能在各個成長階段都茁壯，完成這篇。

經由先前的演練後，現在看下整篇範文並聆聽音檔。

The use of other incentives, such as money, toys, or smartphones, to motivate kids to learn things should be discouraged because it is something that should be developed internally. Only an instinctive drive to learn will last long and eventually become a habit that will benefit a person throughout his or her life.

使用其他誘因例如，金錢、玩具或是智慧型手機，來激勵小孩學習事物的念頭是該打消的，因為學習應該是經由內部化的發展而成的。只有內部的驅策來學習才會是長久的，而且最終會變成習慣的養成，使一個人終生受益。

In one of the bestselling books "*The Promise of A Pencil: How ordinary Person Can Create Extraordinary Change*" uncovers the wisdom behind learning and parental education to their kids, although its main theme is not about how to raise a kid. In describing his childhood, the author Adam Braun had the question, like many of us during our teen days, should we be given money if we get high grades or straight As. His request for money as compensation for his high grades was shut down by his father, who stays firm on not giving kids money in return or not indulging their kids with other incentives.

在暢銷書之一的，《一支鉛筆的承諾：一位普通人如何能創造出驚人的改變》，接露了學習背後所蘊藏的智慧和父母對孩童的教育，儘管這本書的主要主題不是關於如何養育一個小孩。在描述他的童年時期時，作者亞當・博朗，也有著如同我們大多數的人在青少年時期中存有的疑問，我們是否應該拿到金錢獎賞，如果我們得到高的分數或是拿到全 A 的成績。他要求金錢作為他拿到高分的獎勵被他的父親所拒絕，因為他父親堅持不給予小孩金錢的獎勵，或是不以其他誘因來寵壞自己的小孩。

Of course, we would wonder why since other parents are rewarding their kids with money, high-tech toys, and video games. Not explaining all what is behind to their kids, his father would say because "Brauns are different". To kids, it is simply too vague and kids would probably see the response as "No, we are not getting anything in return" or "our father just couldn't think a better excuse to persuade us".

當然，我們會思考著為什麼其他的父母會獎勵他們的孩子們金錢、高科技玩具和影視遊樂器。不向孩子解釋背後所隱含的因素，他父親會說因為「博朗家是不同的」。對小孩來說，這太模糊了而且小孩們通常會將這個回應理解成「不，我們沒有得到任何相對應的回報」或是「我們的父親只是想不出更好的理由來說服我們」。

Eventually, as he recalled "we developed an inherent drive to live into the ideals they had defined us". Deep down, his father wants them to hold a higher standard so that they will develop an inherent drive to learn things. Perhaps his father should explain things to their kids or perhaps explanations cannot make kids at that time fully grasp the underlying meanings.

最後，當他回想起「我們該由本能驅策來實踐出父母所定義我們的理想」。在心底，他的父親想要他們抱持著更高的標準，這樣一來他們就能發展出自動自發的本能去學習事情。或許他的父親應該要向他的孩子解釋事情脈絡又或許解釋並不能使得該年紀的孩子們全然理解父親用意的潛在意圖。

In life, we should develop an inherent drive to learn things so that we can continually survive through the hard times of our life even after we are not in school anymore. Parents simply cannot always reward us something to motive us. People relying on incentives to learn things will encounter a huge setback if there are no incentives, and most people cannot perform well when they enter the job market simply because sometimes there are no incentives. To kids and parents, getting higher grades are important, but what's more important is to look at what's behind it. Only by letting kids develop a high standard and an inherent drive to learn can they thrive in every phase of their lives, even if there are no parental guidance or parental support.

在生命中，我們應該要發展出內在驅策學習事物的能力，這樣我們才能在我們生命艱苦時候，持續生存下去，即使我們不在學校環境了。父母不可能總是因為我們做了什麼事就藉由獎勵我們來驅策我們前進。仰賴誘因學習事物的人，如果在沒有任何誘因存在時會遭遇巨大的挫折，而且大多數的人沒有辦法在步入職場後有良好的表現，因為有時候職場中不會有誘因驅策你。對於小孩和父母來說，獲得較高的分數是重要的，但是更重要的是要能看到背後所隱藏的部分。只有讓小孩發展出高的標準且有本能驅策學習的能力才能讓孩子們在他們人生的每個階段都能茁壯成長，即使當下沒有父母的指導或支持。

UNIT 02

工作類話題①：
工作滿意度和
工作偏好？

TASK 2 Independent Writing

Directions

Read the question below. You have 30 minutes to plan, write, and revise your essay. Typically, an effective response will contain a minimum of 300 words.

TOPIC

Job satisfaction is extremely important in the workplace. Some people deem certain types of work, such as clerical work as something repetitive, and they find that work mundane and boring. They would prefer to do something adventurous and challenging. Doing different types of projects in a single workday gives them energy and a sense of fulfillment. What do you think about this? Use specific reasons and examples to support your answer.

整合能力強化① 實際演練 ▶ *MP3 003*

請自己動手演練並於 30 分鐘內完成至少 300 字的英文文章，盡量以打字的方式進行，因為新托福測驗是電腦考試。

_____

_____

_____

_____

_____

_____

_____

_____

_____

_____

_____

_____

_____

_____

_____

_____

_____

_____

整合能力強化② 單句中譯英演練

在掌握文法句型後,學習者大多能拿到 25 分左右的寫作成績,英語句型多樣性和各式句型是獲取 25⁺高分的關鍵,現在請演練接下來的單句中譯英練習。請務必演練後再觀看答案,並於觀看答案後仔細聆聽音檔,強化對各句型的記憶。

① 在工作場所中的滿意度是非常難衡量和評估的,這真的因人而異。有時候這關係到一個人的個性、產業的類型或是工作內容的熟練度。

_____

_____

【參考答案】

Satisfaction in the workplace is very hard to measure and evaluate, and it really varies from person to person. Sometimes it is related to the personality of the worker, the type of industry, or dexterity of the job content.

② 一方面,不同類型的任務可能給予一個人足夠的空間,能在一項任務和下一項任務中轉換而不感到無趣,但是這有時候可能會使腦部承受不住進而造成許多憂慮和壓力。

_____

_____

【參考答案】

On the one hand, different types of tasks may give a person enough room to shift from doing one task to another without feeling bored, but it can sometimes overwhelm the brain and create lots of anxiety and stress.

③ 做相似的任務，另一方面，給予工作者不需要過度思考的舒適度，但是單調且重複的不斷重複地做同樣類型的任務，可能會導致特定類型的工作者，缺乏足夠的動機去執行任務。

_____

_____

【參考答案】

Doing similar tasks, on the other hand, gives workers the ease of not having to think too much, but monotony and repetition of doing the same tasks over and over can result in a lack of enough motivation to do the task for a certain type of people.

④ 而個性似乎在人們對於工作環境中感到的滿意度分數上扮演著關鍵的角色，當中也有其他的因素牽涉在其中。

_____

_____

【參考答案】

Whereas personality seems to play a pivotal role in the score in the satisfaction people may feel in the workplace, there are other factors involved.

⑤ 不同類型的產業和不同的工作會影響工作者是否必須整天做重複性的任務或是能享有在一天中做不同類型任務的彈性。

_____

_____

Different types of the industry and different jobs will influence whether workers have to do repetitive tasks all day or have to enjoy the flexibility of doing various tasks in a single day.

⑥ 例如,一位攝影師可能會對於整天拍攝一個人感到冗長且無趣,但是多樣化的攝影,包含著模特兒和動物或是模特兒和景點夾雜在其中,就能使攝影師感到有趣且愉快。

_____

_____

For example, a photographer might find shooting a person all day tedious and boring, but the variety of the shooting, which includes animals with models, or models with scenery sandwiched in between, fun and enjoyable.

⑦ 在國際模特兒這個行業的攝影可能給予攝影師更多的自由和不同的任務,因此那些意圖要做些不同且具挑戰性任務的攝影師,就應該要找尋能賦予他們多樣性任務的行業,這樣他們才能夠在工作中感到滿意且長期留任,比起無法給予他們更多工作彈性的工作崗位待上更久。

_____

_____

Photography in the international modeling industry may give photographers more freedom and various tasks, so photographers with the personality of intending to do something different and challenging should find the industry that will give them the variety so that they can feel satisfied with the work and retain at the job longer than in the industry which does not give them freedom.

⑧ 最後，對於工作內容的熟練度，一個人是否能夠找尋不同類型的任務和相似的任務而感到滿意。

_____

_____

【參考答案】
Finally, dexterity of the job content influences whether a person will find different types of tasks and similar tasks satisfying.

⑨ 對於工作內容有一定熟練度的工作者，能以最短路徑執行所有任務。

_____

_____

【參考答案】
People with certain dexterity of the job content will have a short-cut to do all the tasks.

整合能力強化③ 段落拓展

Job satisfaction is extremely important in the workplace. Some people deem certain types of work, such as clerical work as something repetitive, and they find that work mundane and boring. They would prefer to do something adventurous and challenging. Doing different types of projects in a single workday gives them energy and a sense of fulfillment. What do you think about this? Use specific reasons and examples to support your answer.

Step 1 　　進一步探討原因，提出對於題目論述的論點。

　　　　　　（題目中提到了兩種類型的工作：工作內容是重複性高的工作和具冒險性和挑戰性的工作，每個人對於工作的偏好不同，範文中提出了令人省思的問題，並進一步探討影響「工作滿意度」的因素，對於該題目有更好掌握度和 facts 的考生，可以選擇像範文中的敘述句做開頭）。

Step 2 　　先寫出鋪陳的句子後，列出了三個主要原因：一個人的個性、產業的類型或是工作內容的熟練度都影響著工作滿意度。接著概括講述著為何同個條件下，工作滿意度會是因人而異，還有提到工作的重複性。（這三個因素是相互影響的，其實可以探討的部分太廣，可能一篇托福文章也寫

42

不完，考生也可以藉由打工或大學企業工讀中的工作經驗回推，當下就不會不知道要寫什麼了。）

Step 3　接著探討其中**兩個因素「個性」和「產業類型」**，在工作滿意度中扮演的角色，並提到當中也有其他的因素牽涉在其中。不同類型的產業和不同的工作會影響著工作滿意度，然後舉攝影師為例，如果需要工作能賦予更多樣化任務者就更需要選擇像是國際性的模特兒公司等等。工作中有更多彈性，讓個性不喜歡單調或重複性高的攝影師，有更高的留任率。

Step 4　接著提到**「工作的熟練度」**，簡短敘述後，談到難以去界定等，然後提到另一個關鍵因素「心情」。

Step 5　最後總結出要深入探討三個主要的標準：工作者的個性、產業的類型和工作內容的熟練度。只有在結合出工作者在心中如何評定這標準，我們才能探討出工作者是否對於不同類型的任務或相似的任務感到滿意。

經由先前的演練後，現在看下整篇範文並聆聽音檔。

Satisfaction in the workplace is very hard to measure and evaluate, and it really varies from person to person. Sometimes it is related to the personality of the worker, the type of industry, or dexterity of the job content. On the one hand, different types of tasks may give a person enough room to shift from doing one task to another without feeling bored, but it can sometimes overwhelm the brain and create lots of anxiety and stress. Doing similar tasks, on the other hand, gives workers the ease of not having to think too much, but monotony and repetition of doing the same tasks over and over can result in a lack of enough motivation to do the task for a certain type of people. People like sales reps may be the representation of the type who do not want to sit in the office all day doing the same thing.

在工作場所中的滿意度是非常難衡量和評估的，這真的因人而異。有時候這關係到一個人的個性、產業的類型或是工作內容的熟練度。一方面，不同類型的任務可能給予一個人足夠的空間，能在一項任務和下一項任務中轉換而不感到無趣，但是這有時候可能會使腦部承受不住進而造成許多憂慮和壓力。做相似的任務，另一方面，給予工作者不需要過度思考的舒適度，但是單調且重複的不斷重複地做同樣類型的任務，可能會導致特定類型的工作者，缺乏足夠的動機去執行任務。像是業務銷售人員可能就是不想要整天待在辦公室做同樣事情的類型人物代表。

Whereas personality seems to play a pivotal role in the score in the satisfaction people may feel in the workplace, there are other factors involved. Different types of the industry and different jobs will influence whether workers have to do repetitious tasks all day or have to enjoy the flexibility of doing various tasks in a single day. For example, a photographer might find shooting a person all day tedious and boring, but the variety of the shooting, which includes animals with models, or models with scenery sandwiched in between, fun and enjoyable.

而個性似乎在人們對於工作環境中感到的滿意度分數上扮演著關鍵的角色，當中也有其他的因素牽涉在其中。不同類型的產業和不同的工作會影響工作者是否必須整天做重複性的任務或是能享有在一天中做不同類型任務的彈性。例如，一位攝影師可能會對於整天拍攝一個人感到冗長且無趣，但是多樣化的攝影，包含著模特兒和動物或是模特兒和景點夾雜在其中，就能使攝影師感到有趣且感到愉快。因此，攝影師會對於有著不同類型的任務感到滿意。

Therefore, photographers will feel more satisfied with different tasks. Photography in the international modeling industry may give photographers more freedom and various tasks, so photographers with the personality of intending to do something different and challenging should find the industry that will give them the variety so that they can feel satisfied with the work and retain at the job longer than in the industry which does not give them freedom.

在國際模特兒這個行業的攝影可能給予攝影師更多的自由和不同的任務，因此那些意圖要做些不同且具挑戰性任務的攝影師，就應該要找尋能賦予他們多樣性任務的行業，這樣他們才能夠在工作中感到滿意且長期留任，比起無法給予他們更多工作彈性的工作崗位待上更久。

Finally, dexterity of the job content influences whether a person will find different types of tasks and similar tasks satisfying. People with certain dexterity of the job content will have a short-cut to do all the tasks. Therefore, it is hard to define whether they will enjoy different tasks more, and sometimes it is about the mood.

最後，對於工作內容的熟練度，一個人是否能夠找尋不同類型的任務和相似的任務而感到滿意。對於工作內容有一定熟練度的工作者，能以最短路徑執行所有任務。因此，很難去界定工作者是否較喜愛不同類型的任務，而且有時侯心情才是關鍵。

To sum up, we have to take an in-depth look into three major criteria: personality of the worker, type of industry, and dexterity of the job content. Only after combining how workers rate the criteria in the mind can we really talk about whether workers are more satisfied when they have many different types of tasks or similar tasks.

總結來說，我們必須要深入探討三個主要的標準：工作者的個性、產業的類型和工作內容的熟練度。只有在結合出工作者在心中如何評定這標準，我們才能探討出工作者是否對於不同類型的任務或相似的任務感到滿意。

Part 1
獨立篇

Part 2
整合篇

教育類話題②：
父母教育小孩的方式影響孩子
成長和自我探索

 TASK 2 Independent Writing

Directions

Read the question below. You have 30 minutes to plan, write, and revise your essay. Typically, an effective response will contain a minimum of 300 words.

TOPIC

Parents in different districts or various nations will tend to favor a certain approach to raising and educating their kids. Some prefer to spend most of the time taking their kids traveling, exercising in the park, or visiting museums so that their children can develop their own interests along the way. Others are inclined to set a strict rule for their own kids, learning things solely related to school tests or the college entrance exam. What is your opinion on this topic?

整合能力強化① 實際演練 ▶ *MP3 005*

請自己動手演練並於 30 分鐘內完成至少 300 字的英文文章，盡量以打字的方式進行，因為新托福測驗是電腦考試。

_____

_____

_____

_____

_____

_____

_____

_____

_____

_____

_____

_____

_____

_____

整合能力強化② 單句中譯英演練

　　在掌握文法句型後，學習者大多能拿到 25 分左右的寫作成績，英語句型多樣性和各式句型是獲取 25⁺高分的關鍵，現在請演練接下來的單句中譯英練習。請務必演練後再觀看答案，並於觀看答案後仔細聆聽音檔，強化對各句型的記憶。

① 最佳的時間利用是否該花在玩遊戲或運動上或是家庭作業上，一直以來是備受爭論的，但是主要的焦點應該要設定在真正了解你的孩子。

_____

_____

【參考答案】

Whether the best use of the time should be spent on playing games or sports or homework has long been debated, but the main focus should be set on "really understand your kids".

② 即使有著每週聚集在晚餐的集會，小孩還是能隱藏他們的情感，在表面上僅分享出在學校中所發生的正面事物。

_____

_____

【參考答案】

Even if there is a weekly gathering at the dinner table, kids can hide their emotions, and on the surface only sharing all the positive things happening in school.

③ 父母能做的就是將有限的時間花費在與小孩子玩遊戲或運動上，尤其這是他們感到放鬆的時候，但若是將時間花費在學校作業上則可能僅有不好的成果，導致更多的家庭紛爭。

【參考答案】

What parents can do is to spend their limited time playing games or sports with them, especially it is the time they feel relaxed, but spending time doing schoolwork with them can bring only bad outcomes, resulting in more family feuds.

④ 他們不會說些傷人的話，而且同學和孩子處於相同的處境，仍在試圖解決一些數學問題或正開始準備 SAT 測驗，而父母因為自己已經有了相關經驗，表現會優於他們的孩子。

【參考答案】

They won't say something hurtful, and classmates are sometimes in the same situation, still figuring out some math problems or starting to prepare the SAT, whereas parents outperform their kids because they have done those things before.

⑤ 由於父母不是學校作業時間的好人選，他們能做的事是與小孩子玩遊戲或從事運動活動。

Since parents are not good candidates for the schoolwork time, they should instead play games or sports with kids.

⑥ 所有這些事情都是父母在從事學校作業時候無法察覺的，這比起小孩的數學成績或是小孩在拼字比賽中的表現多好，更加重要。

_____

_____

All these are things that parents won't find during schoolwork time, and it is something more important than how well kids do in math or how well kids perform at the spelling bees.

⑦ 其中之一的主婦，麗奈特・思嘉夫在第一季時有四個小孩。有次他對著警察宣洩著自己的情緒「我有四個年紀六歲以下的小孩要養育。我當然會有情緒控管問題。」，但是她卻也展示出一些與這主題相關的部分。

_____

_____

One of the housewives, Lynette Scavo has four kids in season one. One time she vented her emotions to the policeman that "I have four kids under the age of six. I absolutely have anger management issues", but she also demonstrates something related to the topic.

⑧ 藉由與她的小孩玩棒球，她展現出她的耐心，即使她開玩笑說：
如果我把棒球再丟慢些，那就是在打保齡球了。

_____

_____

【參考答案】
By playing baseball with her kid, she shows her patience even though she laughs like if I threw a little slower, then I would be playing bowing.

⑨ 小孩在乎著，當他們本身正對於學習某些事情感到掙扎時，父母是否能夠對他們表現出耐心，但大多數的父母卻是相反的做法，將小孩推的離他們更遠了。

_____

_____

【參考答案】
Kids care about whether parents can show patience to them when they are obviously struggling to learn things, and most of the time parents are doing the opposite pushing their kids further away from them.

Parents in different districts or various nations will tend to favor a certain approach to raising and educating their kids. Some prefer to spend most of the time taking their kids traveling, exercising in the park, or visiting museums so that their children can develop their own interests along the way. Others are inclined to set a strict rule for their own kids, learning things solely related to school tests or the college entrance exam. What is your opinion on this topic?

Step 1 父母會選擇教育孩子的方式很多，看完題目後可以先思考一下要如何構思這篇文章，題目中提到的兩個方向是不同的，一個偏向讓小孩經由去博物館等活動探索自我，而另一種則偏向傳統型教育模式。

Step 2 範文的開頭點出先要了解孩子，才能逐步思考出到底什麼方式會更適合孩子，接著指出「**主要的焦點應該要設定在真正了解你的孩子**」並進一步闡述。

Step 3 用對比的方式陳述出「父母」扮演的角色和「教師、同班同學、親密朋友和家教」之間的不同，並說明父母若把時間花在遊戲和運動上，則家庭更和樂。（父母的相關經驗或考試經驗已經先入為主的影響孩子學習，但孩子並非父母本身，且每個人學習情況不同，反推回去會造成親子關係不佳。）

Step 4　次個段落繼續針對前個段落中的重點進一步說明，首句就引入主題「由於父母不是學校作業時間的好人選，他們能做的事是，應該與小孩子玩遊戲或從事運動活動。」。**緊接著接續提問，讓讀者反思。於接續的問句後再次講述與孩子遊戲或運動的優點，且這遠比分數重要多了。**

Step 5　最後的段落提到《慾望師奶》中小孩教養的部分和智慧，除了能引起考官或讀者共鳴外，也能提升說服力，並由當中教育孩子的部分，進一步強化立場達到說服效果。**生動的表明出劇中教育孩子的部分也是加分點，能與坊間範文或其他考生的回答作出區隔，一舉獲取高分。**

經由先前的演練後,現在看下整篇範文並聆聽音檔。

Whichever approach parents choose, the main focus should be set on "really understand your kids". Understanding kids can be quite hard simply because kids don't always tell you everything. Even if there is a weekly gathering at the dinner table, kids can hide their emotions, and on the surface only sharing all the positive things happening in school.

不論父母選擇哪種方法,主要的焦點應該要設定在真正了解你的孩子。了解孩子可能相當困難僅因為孩子不會總是告訴你每件事。即使有著每週聚集在晚餐的集會,小孩還是能隱藏他們的情感,在表面上僅分享出在學校中所發生的正面事物。

What parents can do is to spend their limited time playing games or sports with them, especially it is the time they feel relaxed, but spending time doing schoolwork with them can bring only bad outcomes, resulting in more family feuds. Teachers, classmates, close friends, and tutors can be the better person than parents to do the schoolwork time. They won't say something hurtful, and classmates are sometimes in the same situation, still figuring out some math problems or starting to prepare the SAT, whereas parents outperform their kids because they have done those things before.

父母能做的就是將有限的時間花費在與小孩子玩遊戲或運動上，尤其這是他們感到放鬆的時候，但若是將時間花費在學校作業上則可能僅有不好的成果，導致更多的家庭紛爭。教師、同班同學、親密朋友和指導員比起父母能扮演著在學習上更好的角色。他們不會說些傷人的話，而且同學和孩子處於相同的處境，仍在試圖解決一些數學問題或正開始準備 SAT 測驗，而父母因為自己已經有了相關經驗，表現會優於他們的孩子。

Since parents are not good candidates for the schoolwork time, they should instead play games or sports with kids. It is the time they can understand their kids, like how kids think about the strategy of playing football and why they think that way or how they cooperate with siblings, friends, family members, or are kids a good team player? Or how kids crack the puzzle? All these are things that parents won't find during schoolwork time, and it is something more important than how well my kids do in math or how well kids perform at the spelling bees. It is something that will shape their character and personality. It is something that builds the bond between parents and kids.

由於父母不是學校作業時間的好人選，他們能做的事是與小孩子玩遊戲或從事運動活動。這是他們能夠了解孩子的時候，像是小孩是如何思考玩足球的策略和為什麼他們會這樣思考或是他們如何與兄弟姊妹、朋友、家庭成員合作或是小孩是個良好的團隊合作者嗎?或是小孩是如何解開謎團的呢？所有這些事情都是父母在從事學校作業時候無法察覺的，這比起小孩的數學成績或是小孩在拼字比賽中的表現多好，更加重要。這是形塑他們角色和個性的時候。這也是父母和小孩們建議情感連結的時候。

In one of the successful sitcoms, *Desperate Housewives*, it uncovers some wisdom of how parents raise kids or how four housewives raise kids. It is something the audience can learn from. One of the housewives, Lynette Scavo has four kids in season one. One time she vented her emotions to the policeman that "I have four kids under the age of six. I absolutely have anger management issues", but she also demonstrates something related to the topic. She does spend time with her kids by playing sports even if her husband says their kid is not the baseball material so he doesn't have to play.

在一部成功的影集之一《慾望師奶》中，它揭露了一些父母如何養育小孩或是四個主婦如何養育小孩的智慧。這是一些觀眾們能夠學習的部分。其中之一的主婦，麗奈特・思嘉夫在第一季時有四個小孩。有次他對著警察宣洩著自己的情緒「我有四個年紀六歲以下的小孩要養育。我當然會有情緒控管問題。」，但是她卻也展示出一些與這主題相關的部分。她花費時間與小孩們從事運動活動，即使她丈夫表明著他們小孩不是打棒球的料，所以他不需要練棒球。

By playing baseball with her kid, she shows her patience even though she laughs like if I threw a little slower, then I would be playing bowing. She wants her kid to have the personality to not quit doing things, and most important of all she understands her kid. Kids need that kind of support. Kids care about whether parents can show patience to them when they are obviously struggling to learn things, and most of the time parents are doing the opposite pushing their kids further away from them. So from above-mentioned reasons, I prefer to let kids do several activities so that they can explore themselves and can find their own interests.

藉由與她的小孩玩棒球，她展現出她的耐心，即使她開玩笑說：如果我把棒球再丟慢些，那就是在打保齡球了。她想要自己的小孩能夠有著做事不放棄的個性，最重要的是她了解她的小孩。孩子們需要那樣的情感支持。孩子們在乎著，當他們本身正對於學習某些事情感到掙扎時，他們的父母是否能夠對他們表現出耐心，但大多數的父母卻是相反的做法，將小孩推的離他們更遠了。所以從上述的這些理由，我偏好讓小孩從事各種活動，這樣一來他們能夠探索自我，找到他們自己的興趣。

UNIT
04

教育類話題③：
父母教育影響小孩
作決定和獨立

 TASK 2 Independent Writing

Directions

Read the question below. You have 30 minutes to plan, write, and revise your essay. Typically, an effective response will contain a minimum of 300 words.

TOPIC

Decision making is quite essential in our lives, but nowadays parents tend to be the ones who are responsible for kids' inability to make major decisions and be independent. People from the previous generation; however, had no trouble making a major decision. What do you think about these statements?

整合能力強化① 實際演練 ▶ *MP3 007*

請自己動手演練並於 30 分鐘內完成至少 300 字的英文文章，盡量以打字的方式進行，因為新托福測驗是電腦考試。

整合能力強化② 單句中譯英演練

　　在掌握文法句型後，學習者大多能拿到 25 分左右的寫作成績，英語句型多樣性和各式句型是獲取 25⁺高分的關鍵，現在請演練接下來的單句中譯英練習。請務必演練後再觀看答案，並於觀看答案後仔細聆聽音檔，強化對各句型的記憶。

① 校園環境是衡量學生是否有能力自立和能夠對於他們自己本身生活做出重大決定的指標之一。

　　_____

　　_____

【參考答案】

Campus settings are one of the indicators to measure whether or not students are able to stand on their own feet and are able to make major decisions for their own life.

② 不同於在《你如何衡量你的人生》一書中所描述的足球父母們，會替他們的小孩安排太多事情，現今的父母們過於保護自己的孩子。他們總是擔憂著他們。

　　_____

　　_____

【參考答案】

Unlike what is described in *How Will You Measure Your Life*, the soccer parents, who arranged too many things for their kids, today's parents are too protective of their kids. They are constantly worried about them.

③ 在學校裡，父母不是從遠距離的地方拜訪他們的小孩，卻是從事著替小孩們清掃的工作。

_____

_____

【參考答案】

On campus, parents are not visiting their kids from a far distance but doing the cleaning for their kids.

④ 有位學校校長回憶，接到數通來自父母的電話，關於學校政策不適合他們的孩子。

_____

_____

【參考答案】

One headmaster recalled getting calls from parents about school policies not quite suitable for their kids.

⑤ 或是教授接到父母的電話，告知他們的小孩需要請假。

_____

_____

【參考答案】

Or professors getting calls from parents that their kids want to take a leave of absence.

⑥ 年輕人替自己做決定的能力不是稍微退步些，而是有大幅度的退步，根據許多教授的陳述。

_____

_____

【參考答案】
Young people's ability to make decisions is not just regressing for a bit, but quite a lot, according to many professors.

⑦ 你如何能期待孩子做重大的決定，當孩子們連像是向教授請假這些微不足道的小事都需要父母代勞呢？

_____

_____

【參考答案】
How can you expect kids to make major decisions about life when they cannot make something as trivial as asking for a leave of absence to professors in person.

⑧ 其他教授甚至接到來自父母的來電，告知他們既然這是知名的大學，在競爭上會異常激烈，他們不希望看到他們小孩的自尊受到傷害。

_____

_____

【參考答案】

Other professors even get calls from parents informing them that since it's a well-known university, competition is so fierce that they don't want to see their kids' feelings getting hurt.

⑨ 年輕人卻束手無策因為他們已經適應了從母親子宮出生後，父母都會替他們打算的日子了。

_____

_____

【參考答案】

Young people can do nothing about it simply because they have accustomed to what their parents will do for them right after they come out of mother's womb.

⑩ 這已經成了習慣，父母們會做像是替他們打掃這樣子微不足道的小事到替他們撰寫履歷和打電話給公司的人事專員。

_____

_____

【參考答案】

It has become a habit that their parents will do things as trivial as cleaning to something as major as writing a resume and making a phone call to the company's HR personnel.

Decision making is quite essential in our lives, but nowadays parents tend to be the ones who are responsible for kids' inability to make major decisions and be independent. People from the previous generation; however, had no trouble making a major decision. What do you think about these statements?

Step 1　看完題目後先寫出概述句，定義出「在校園環境是衡量學生是否有能力自立和能夠對於他們自己本身生活做出重大決定的指標之一。」，這段於後面要寫出題目中提到的「孩子更難獨立跟做決定等」是相關聯的，也更好去延伸段落。

Step 2　選擇好立場後，列出陳述句後緊接著表明事情並非如此，並使用《你如何衡量你的人生》一書中所描述的足球父母們，強化不同意的立場，過度替小孩安排事情的足球父母，造成了小孩子過於依賴等問題，除了呼應首句，也為下個段落作了鋪陳。

Step 3　舉出實例，包含校長和教授接到電話的部分，還有使用誇飾「年輕人替自己做決定的能力不是稍微退步些，而是有

大幅度的退步，根據許多教授的陳述。」還有反問等接續對不同意這個論點進行論述，清楚點出不同意的原因。這些都導致了年輕人無法替自己的人生做出重大的決定。

Step 4 最後一段更詼諧地描述「跟過去年輕人相比，現今的年輕人就像是溫室的玫瑰。年輕人卻束手無策因為他們已經適應了從母親子宮出生後，父母都會替他們打算的日子了。」。「這已經成了習慣，父母們會做像是替他們打掃這樣子微不足道的小事到替他們撰寫履歷和打電話給公司的人事專員。」最後以因為這些因素所以不同意題目論述作為結束。

經由先前的演練後，現在看下整篇範文並聆聽音檔。

Campus settings are one of the indicators to measure whether or not students are able to stand on their own feet and are able to make major decisions for their own life. Recently, what has been observed by reporters, professors, and school headmasters shows this has never been the case. Students are too reliant on their parents to make decisions for them. Unlike what is described in *How Will You Measure Your Life*, the soccer parents, who arranged too many things for their kids, today's parents are too protective of their kids. They are constantly worried about them.

校園環境是衡量學生是否有能力自立和能夠對於他們自己本身生活做出重大決定的指標之一。最近，記者們、教授們和學校校長們卻表示，事實並非如此。學生太依賴父母來替他們做出決定。不同於在《你如何衡量你的人生》一書中所描述的足球父母們，會替他們的小孩安排太多事情，現今的父母們過於保護自己的孩子。他們總是擔憂著他們。

On campus, parents are not visiting their kids from a far distance but doing the cleaning for their kids. One headmaster recalled getting calls from parents about school policies not quite suitable for their kids, or professors getting calls from parents that their kids want to take a leave of absence. Something is going wrong in the campus. Young people's ability to make decisions is not just regressing for a bit, but quite a lot, according to many professors. How can you expect kids to make major decisions about life when they cannot make something as trivial as asking for a leave of absence to professors in person.

在學校裡，父母不是從遠距離的地方拜訪他們的小孩，卻是從事著替小孩們清掃的工作。有位學校校長回憶，接到數通來自父母的電話，關於學校政策不適合他們的孩子。或是教授接到父母的電話，告知他們的小孩需要請假。在校園中顯然這些事情不太對。年輕人替自己做決定的能力不是稍微退步些，而是有大幅度的退步，根據許多教授的陳述。你如何能期待孩子做重大的決定，當孩子們連像是向教授請假的這些微不足道的小事都需要父母代勞呢？

Other professors even get calls from parents informing them that since it's a well-known university, competition is so fierce that they don't want to see their kids' feelings getting hurt. Parents' interference and over protection is one of the reasons harming today's young people, resulting in not being able to make decisions for their own life.

其他教授甚至接到來自父母的來電，告知他們既然這是知名的大學，在競爭上會異常激烈，他們不希望看到他們小孩的自尊受到傷害。父母的干預和過度的保護是傷害現今年輕人的原因之一，導致年輕人無法替自己的人生做出重大的決定。

Today's young people are like roses in a greenhouse, compared with young people in the past. Young people can do nothing about it simply because they have accustomed to what their parents will do for them right after they come out of mother's womb. It has become a habit that their parents will do things as trivial as cleaning to something as major as writing a resume and making a phone call to the company's HR personnel. Some parents even go to the interview with their kids and doing all the talking. All these make interviewers not convince candidates' ability to do the job. From all these reasons, perhaps today's parents should dial back to how parents raised kids from the previous generations so that kids can develop a sound mindset and decision-making ability. Therefore, I think these statements are so true.

跟過去年輕人相比，現今的年輕人就像是溫室的玫瑰。年輕人卻束手無策因為他們已經適應了從母親子宮出生後，父母都會替他們打算的日子了。這已經成了習慣，父母們會做像是替他們打掃這樣子微不足道的小事到替他們撰寫履歷和打電話給公司的人事專員。有些父母甚至陪同小孩去參加面試，而且全程都替小孩子回答。這些都讓面試官們質疑候選人有做這份工作的能力。從這些原因來看，或許今日的父母應該要將事情撥回正軌，撥回至上一代父母如何養育小孩，這樣他們的小孩才能夠發展出健全的心態且具備做決定的能力。因此，我認為這些陳述是很真實的。

NOTE

UNIT 05

教育類話題④：
名人言行對
年輕人的影響

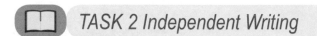

📖 *TASK 2 Independent Writing*

Directions

Read the question below. You have 30 minutes to plan, write, and revise your essay. Typically, an effective response will contain a minimum of 300 words.

TOPIC

Some people proclaim that actions of young people are easily influenced by celebrities, and it is not a good thing. Others think the influence of celebrities on young people can be quite positive and inspiring. What is your opinion?

整合能力強化① 實際演練 ▶ *MP3 009*

請自己動手演練並於 30 分鐘內完成至少 300 字的英文文章，盡量以打字的方式進行，因為新托福測驗是電腦考試。

_____

_____

_____

_____

_____

_____

_____

_____

_____

_____

_____

_____

_____

_____

_____

_____

整合能力強化② 單句中譯英演練

在掌握文法句型後，學習者大多能拿到 25 分左右的寫作成績，英語句型多樣性和各式句型是獲取 25⁺高分的關鍵，現在請演練接下來的單句中譯英練習。請務必演練後再觀看答案，並於觀看答案後仔細聆聽音檔，強化對各句型的記憶。

① 年輕人，不論他們是青少年、剛從大學畢業的畢業生或是剛進入職場工作幾年的人，都深受到名人的影響。

_____

_____

【參考答案】

Young people, whether they are just teenagers, new grads, or people who just entered the workplace for a few years, are deeply influenced by celebrities.

② 不論他們正經歷人生的哪個階段，他們都迫切需要榜樣。他們的心智是如此混亂以至於他們需要有他們能夠尊崇的人。

_____

_____

【參考答案】

No matter what phases they are experiencing, they are in desperate need of the role model.

③ 名人不會對年輕人的生活做出干涉而且他們不會做出批評。

_____

_____

【參考答案】

Celebrities will not interfere young people's life, and they will not judge.

④ 例如，代言的名人如果是健康且鼓勵人心的，就能對於喜歡那些名人的年輕人產生正面的影響。

_____

_____

【參考答案】

For example, spokespersons who are healthy and encouraging can have a positive effect on those young people who like them.

⑤ 年輕人會想要讓自己像那些名人，所以他們會改善自己的健康，這樣他們就能夠看起來像那些超級巨星了。

_____

_____

【參考答案】

Young people want to look like them, so they want to improve their health so that they can look like those superstars.

⑥ 他們讀著超級巨星的童年故事和許多事情。他們能夠產生共鳴且對於他們自己本身能夠產生相似的投影作用。

_____

_____

【參考答案】

They read superstars' childhood story and many other things. They resonate and mirror those similar to themselves.

⑦ 例如，如果一位超級巨星有著可怕的童年而且過去常因為本身的體重受到嘲笑，進而驅使自己改善至現今天體態，年輕人就能立即的產生共鳴。

_____

_____

【參考答案】

For example, if a superstar who had a horrible childhood and used to get made fun of her weight keeps improving herself to what she is today, young people can immediately relate to her.

⑧ 他們會受到內部化的驅策，而且某些程度上能夠減輕自己心中所產生的痛處，像是"終於有個人能夠知道我在經歷什麼了。"

_____

_____

【參考答案】

They are internally motivated, and somehow eases their pain inside their hearts, like finally someone really knows what I am going through.

⑨ 年輕人若不遵守父母和教師的建議，則會立即被標籤成反叛和不遵守規定。

_____

_____

【參考答案】

Young people who do not follow what parents or teachers suggest can soon be labelled as rebellious and disobedient.

⑩ 既然年輕人有著像是自我認同的危機，他們更易受到名人的影響，也因此對他們而言，名人對於年輕人來說比對年長者更重要。

_____

_____

【參考答案】

Since young people have problems like self-identity crisis, they are more likely to be influenced by celebrities and therefore, to them, celebrities are more important to young people than they are to old people.

Some people proclaim that actions of young people are easily influenced by celebrities, and it is not a good thing. Others think the influence of celebrities on young people can be quite positive and inspiring. What is your opinion?

Step 1 先思考「年輕人的行為真的容易受到名人的影響嗎」以及「名人對於年輕人的影響可以是相當正面且激勵人心的」。

Step 2 範文中定義出在某些人生階段，年輕人是容易受到名人影響的，並點出原因，因為年輕人需要一個榜樣。

（年輕人面對著求職等考驗，其實內心很需要指南針，有位正面且能適時導引年輕人思考的名人，就會有 fans 且能持續影響著年輕人。）

Step 3 次個段落寫到名人會受到尊崇的原因，也提到正面影響和投影作用。除了讓年輕人就能立即的產生共鳴外，他們會受到內部化的驅策，而且某些程度上能夠減輕自己心中所產生的痛處。年輕人最終是希望有人能懂自己，像是"終於有個人能夠知道我在經歷什麼了。"

Part 1
獨立篇

Part 2
整合篇

Step 4　下個段落提到為什麼父母和師長較難扮演這樣的角色，所以名人更容易發揮作用。

（父母的角色等，很容易在提出建議時，造成更多的衝突。）

Step 5　提到年輕人有自我認同的危機等，並對比年輕人和年長者，名人顯然對於年長者的影響較小。

Step 6　最後總結出名人對於年輕人來說，影響是很正向的。

經由先前的演練後,現在看下整篇範文並聆聽音檔。

Young people, whether they are just teenagers, new grads, or people who just entered the workplace for a few years, are deeply influenced by celebrities. No matter what phases they are experiencing, they are in desperate need of role models. Their state of mind is so chaotic that they need someone to look up to. Parents, educators, and friends cannot replace the role of celebrities. It is not that those people care less about young people's life. It is about respect and many other things.

年輕人,不論他們是青少年、剛從大學畢業的畢業生或是剛進入職場工作幾年的人,都深受到名人的影響。不論他們正經歷人生的哪個階段,他們都迫切需要榜樣。他們的心智是如此混亂以至於他們需要有他們能夠尊崇的人。父母、教育學家和朋友無法替代名人的角色。並不是這些人對於年輕人的生活較不關心。這是關於尊重和許多其他的事情。

Celebrities will not interfere young people's life, and they will not judge. They represent a certain image for those young people to follow. For example, spokespersons who are healthy and encouraging can have a positive effect on those young people who like them.

Young people want to look like them, so they want to improve their health so that they can look like those superstars.

名人不會對年輕人的生活做出干涉而且他們不會做出批評。他們代表著特定的形象，讓那些年輕人能夠尊崇。例如，代言的名人如果是健康且鼓勵人心的，就能對於喜歡那些名人的年輕人產生正面的影響。年輕人會想要讓自己像那些名人，所以他們會改善自己的健康，這樣他們就能夠看起來像那些超級巨星了。

Encouraging words can also have a significant influence on those young people. They will not need guidance and support from parents and teachers who also say something against. They read superstars' childhood story and many other things. They resonate and mirror those similar to themselves. For example, if a superstar who had a horrible childhood and used to get made fun of her weight keeps improving herself to what she is today, young people can immediately relate to her. They are internally motivated, and somehow eases their pain inside their hearts, like finally someone really knows what I am going through.

鼓勵性的話也能夠對於那些年輕人有很深遠的影響。年輕人不會需要父母和老師的指導和支持，因為他們只會說些反對的話。他們讀著超級巨星的童年故事和許多事情。他們能夠產生共鳴且對於他們自己本身能夠產生相似的投影作用。例如，如果一位超級巨星有著可怕的童年而且過去常因為本身的體重受到嘲笑，進而驅使自己改善至現今天體態，年輕人就能立即的產生共鳴。他們會受到內部化的驅策，而且某些程度上能夠減輕自己心中所產生的痛處，像是"終於有個人能夠知道我在經歷什麼了。"

Parents and teachers, on the other hand, are not doing the right thing. They do not understand their kids. Saying nice words to their kid, who is obviously overweight, will not solve what their children need. Young people who do not follow what parents or teachers suggest can soon be labelled as rebellious and disobedient. Young people's self-identity crisis can only be solved, if parents are really on their side and empathize with their kids' situation.

父母和老師，另一方面，卻並未做對事情。他們不了解自己的小孩。對他們的小孩說些好話，但小孩本身顯然是體重過重，並不能解決小孩需求。年輕人若不遵守父母和教師的建議，則會立即被標籤成反叛和不遵守規定。年輕人的自我認同危機僅能在父母都真的站在他們的處境設想，且對於小孩們的處境有同理心時才得以解決。

Since young people have problems like self-identity crisis, they are more likely to be influenced by celebrities and therefore, to them, celebrities are more important to young people than they are to old people. Old people's life has already been determined. Most of them are married, have jobs, and have children. They are so mature and their age packages them with experiences that young people are clearly lacking. Old people who listen to encouraging words given by celebrities might possibly nodding their heads, agreeing with them, but deep down they have the reactions like, that's what we did when we were 28 or that's how I recovered after I was fired from my first job.

既然年輕人有著像是自我認同的危機，他們更易受到名人的影響，也因此對他們而言，名人對於年輕人來說比對年長者更重要。年長者的生活已經塵埃落定了。大多數的人都結了婚、有工作和有小孩。他們如此的成熟且他們的年紀乘載著經驗，而這些卻是年輕人所欠缺的。年長者聽著名人所講述的鼓勵性的話可能僅是點著頭，同意這些陳述，但心底卻有個像是這就是我之前 28 歲時在做的事或是這就是我如何從第一份工作被解雇後如何平復心情。

From all these reasons, I do think celebrities have a positive effect on young people.

從這些理由看來，我認為名人對於年輕人來說有正向的影響。

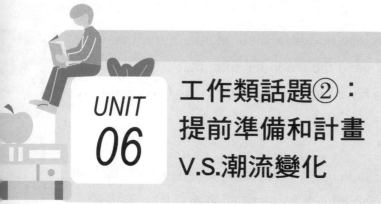

UNIT
06

工作類話題②：
提前準備和計畫
V.S.潮流變化

 TASK 2 Independent Writing

Directions

Read the question below. You have 30 minutes to plan, write, and revise your essay. Typically, an effective response will contain a minimum of 300 words.

TOPIC

In life, we have been told that we should "plan ahead", but others think that planning ahead is not always a good thing since "plans cannot always keep up with changes". The world is changing so fast, and sometimes current trends have become obsolete in a week. What do you think about this?

整合能力強化① 實際演練 ▶ *MP3 011*

請自己動手演練並於 30 分鐘內完成至少 300 字的英文文章，盡量以打字的方式進行，因為新托福測驗是電腦考試。

_____

_____

_____

_____

_____

_____

_____

_____

_____

_____

_____

_____

_____

_____

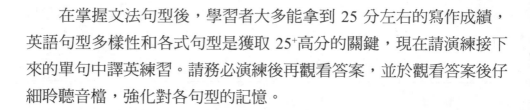

整合能力強化② 單句中譯英演練

在掌握文法句型後，學習者大多能拿到 25 分左右的寫作成績，英語句型多樣性和各式句型是獲取 25⁺高分的關鍵，現在請演練接下來的單句中譯英練習。請務必演練後再觀看答案，並於觀看答案後仔細聆聽音檔，強化對各句型的記憶。

① 在生活中，我們被告知著我們該「提前計畫」或是「在一些事上要贏在起跑點」，但是關乎這些最重要的是要贏在終點。

_____

_____

【參考答案】

In life, we have been told that we should "plan ahead" or "win something at the very beginning", but what matters the most is to win at the end.

② 以計畫和組織為例，對人們來說計畫和組織可以件好事，但是也可以是對於我們造成壞多於好的影響。

_____

_____

【參考答案】

Take planning and organizing for example, planning and organizing can be good things for young people, but it can also be something that does more harm than good.

③ 計畫和組織可能聽起來是個好的想法，但是他們讓人們遵循著太受限定的道路。

_____

_____

【參考答案】

Planning and organizing may sound like a good idea, but they make people follow too rigid a path.

④ 大多數時候，人們不了解自己本身，而且他們計畫了十年大計走在限定的道路上，期許成為某個人或某樣他們認為他們未來會從事的事物或是他們認為他們喜愛的事物。

_____

_____

【參考答案】

Most of the time, people do not know themselves very well, and they plan the 10-year plan for a rigid path to becoming someone or something they think they will be doing or something they deem they love doing it.

⑤ 還是存在著我們可能會感到有興趣的事情。這是因為我們沒有探索足夠的事情來發掘出我們所真正喜愛的。

_____

_____

【參考答案】

There are things we might feel interested in. It is because we do not explore enough things to discover what we truly love.

⑥ 如果年輕人或父母沒有計畫或組織所有事情，年輕人就可以體驗各式各樣的事物，而因此他們對於自己本身會有更好的了解並且找到真正的熱情。

_____

_____

【參考答案】

If young people or parents do not plan and organize all things, young people can experience a variety of things, and therefore they can have a better understanding about themselves and find their true passions.

⑦ 我們無法預測我們的職涯道路。計畫給予我們事情將會如何進行的錯覺，但是這純粹是基於我們的預測。

_____

_____

【參考答案】

We cannot predict our career path. Planning gives us a false sense of how things will go, but it is purely based on our own predication.

⑧ 世界改變的如此快速，以至於我們很難去知道哪些技能在接下來的五年會是主流和趨勢。

_____

_____

【參考答案】

The world is changing so fast that we can hardly know which skills will be mainstream and trendy in the next five years.

⑨ 年輕人應該要做的是盡可能地去嘗試做越多事情越好而且停止對任何他們認為不重要或與他們職涯無關的機會說不。

_____

_____

【參考答案】

What young people should be doing is try as many things as possible and stop saying no to any opportunity that they deem not important or relevant to their career plan or career goal.

⑩ 此外，他們應該要做許多新奇的事情、探索任何他們可能感興趣的事情、自願地做他們不感興趣的事情，跳脫框架思考並且嘗試些稀奇古怪的事情。

_____

_____

【參考答案】

Furthermore, they should do many novel things, explore anything they might be interested in, volunteer to do things they are not interested, think outside of the box, and try something zany.

In life, we have been told that we should "plan ahead", but others think that planning ahead is not always a good thing since "plans cannot always keep up with changes". The world is changing so fast, and sometimes current trends have become obsolete in a week. What do you think about this?

Step 1 題目中提到「plan ahead」和「plans cannot always keep up with changes」，而且流行趨勢變換的非常快速。範文中先點出「關乎這些最重要的是要贏在終點」。

Step 2 緊接著探討的是與「組織和計畫」相對的概念「稀奇古怪」。計畫和組織太限定，逐步拓展段落至這其實對於一個人的發展造成阻礙。未充分了解自我和探索所感興趣的事就先做出一堆計畫，其實對自己造成了很大的影響，讓自己停滯不前。接著講述十年大計並緊接以轉折句講述「然而，人們並非生來就能保持單一的心態。世上還是存在著我們可能會感到有興趣的事情。這是因為我們沒有探索足夠的事情來發掘出我們所真正喜愛的。」。

Step 3　　進一步闡述論點，「**我們的生命軌跡是非限定的**」，並點出事情常不會照著計劃走，和「計畫趕不上變化」。

Step 4　　最後提到世界變遷的部分並做出總結，我認為做些稀奇古怪的事和沿路中探索事物，比起遵循著直線的道路要好得多了。最後的結果可能是很驚人且值得的。

Part 1
獨立篇

Part 2
整合篇

經由先前的演練後，現在看下整篇範文並聆聽音檔。

In life, we have been told that we should "plan ahead" or "win something at the very beginning", but what matters the most is to win at the end. It tells us something about we should take charge of our lives, and not letting the advice confuse what we should be doing. Take planning and organizing for example, planning and organizing can be good things for people, but it can also be something that does more harm than good.

在生活中，我們被告知著我們該「提前計畫」或是「在一些事上要贏在起跑點」，但是關乎這些最重要的是要贏在終點。這告訴我們一些關於我們應該要掌控自己的生活，而且不要讓這些忠告混淆我們應該做的事。以計畫和組織為例，對人們來說計畫和組織可以件好事，但是也可以是對於我們造成壞多於好的影響。

Planning and organizing may sound like a good idea, but they make people follow too rigid a path. People are not doing the right thing in their life. They do not reflect things very often, until years later regretting that they did not do something zany. Not doing something zany impedes a person from developing something great within themselves.

計畫和組織可能聽起來是個好的想法，但是他們讓人們遵循著太受限定的道路。人們在他們的生活中並未做著對的事情。他們通常不思考事情，直到幾年後後悔他們沒有做些稀奇古怪的事。不做些稀奇古怪的事阻礙一個人發展出自己本身中很棒的事。

Part 1
獨立篇

Part 2
整合篇

Most of the time, people do not know themselves very well, and they plan the 10-year plan for a rigid path to becoming someone or something they think they will be doing or something they deem they love doing. However, people are not borne with a straight mindset. There are things we might feel interested in. It is because we do not explore enough things to discover what we truly love. If young people or parents do not plan and organize all things, young people can experience a variety of things, and therefore they can have a better understanding about themselves and find their true passions.

大多數時候，人們不了解自己本身，而且他們計畫了十年大計走在限定的道路上，期許成為某個人或某樣他們認為他們未來會從事的事物或是他們認為他們喜愛的事物。然而，人們並非生來就能保持單一的心態。世上還是存在著我們可能會感到有興趣的事情。這是因為我們沒有探索足夠的事情來發掘出我們所真正喜愛的。如果年輕人或父母沒有計畫或組織所有事情，年輕人就可以體驗各式各樣的事物，而因此他們對於自己本身會有更好的了解並且找到真正的熱情。

In addition, our life trajectory is non-linear. We cannot predict our career path. Planning gives us a false sense of how things will go, but it is purely based on our own predication. It is quite likely that things will not go according to our plan. As a saying goes, "plans cannot always keep up with changes".

此外，我們的生命軌跡是非限定的。我們無法預測我們的職涯道路。計畫給予我們事情將會如何進行的錯覺，但是這純粹是基於我們的預測。事情相當有可能不會照我們的計畫走。有句俗諺說：「計畫趕不上變化」。

The world is changing so fast that we can hardly know which skills will be mainstream and trendy in the next five years. Planning and organizing will make someone follow a too rigid path and lose competitiveness in today's world. What young people should be doing is try as many things as possible and stop saying no to any opportunity that they deem not important or relevant to their career plan or career goal.

世界改變的如此快速，以至於我們很難去知道哪些技能在接下來的五年會是主流和趨勢。計畫和組織會使一個人遵循著太受限定的道路而在現今世界中失去競爭力。年輕人應該要做的是盡可能地去嘗試，做越多事情越好，停止對任何他們認為不重要或與他們職涯無關的機會說不。

Part 1
獨立篇

Part 2
整合篇

Furthermore, they should do many novel things, explore anything they might be interested in, volunteer to do things they are not interested, think outside of the box, and try something zany. From all the above-mentioned descriptions, I think doing something zany and exploring things along the way are better than following a straight line. The outcome can be surprising and rewarding.

此外，他們應該要做許多新奇的事情、探索任何他們可能感興趣的事情、自願地做他們不感興趣的事情，跳脫框架思考並且嘗試些稀奇古怪的事情。從所有上述的描述中，我認為做些稀奇古怪的事和沿路中探索事物，比起遵循著直線的道路要好得多了。最後的結果可能是很驚人且值得的。

UNIT
07

社交類話題①：
友誼的維持和偏好
的交友方式

TASK 2 Independent Writing

Directions

Read the question below. You have 30 minutes to plan, write, and revise your essay. Typically, an effective response will contain a minimum of 300 words.

TOPIC

In our life, we all expect our friendship with other people will remain, but sometimes things do not go as we expected. Some people adopt a more leisure approach by not thinking about friendship; and therefore, are more likely to retain their friendship with others. Others are fixed on maintaining friendship with a certain ritual, thinking that only by following it can friendships last and blossom. What is your opinion?

整合能力強化① 實際演練 ▶ *MP3 013*

請自己動手演練並於 30 分鐘內完成至少 300 字的英文文章，盡量以打字的方式進行，因為新托福測驗是電腦考試。

_____

_____

_____

_____

_____

_____

_____

_____

_____

_____

_____

_____

_____

_____

_____

_____

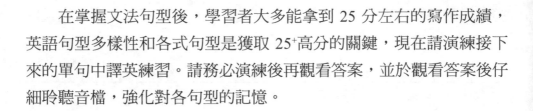

整合能力強化② 單句中譯英演練

　　在掌握文法句型後，學習者大多能拿到 25 分左右的寫作成績，英語句型多樣性和各式句型是獲取 25⁺高分的關鍵，現在請演練接下來的單句中譯英練習。請務必演練後再觀看答案，並於觀看答案後仔細聆聽音檔，強化對各句型的記憶。

① 長時間與朋友們維持一段友誼可能有時候是具有回報的，因為你可以在一路上有一群瞭解你和支持你的朋友，但是這也可能是相當具有傷害性的。

_____

_____

【參考答案】

Maintaining friendship with a small number of people over a long period of time can be rewarding sometimes since you have a group of friends who understand you and support you along the way, but it can sometimes be quite harmful.

② 在生活中，我們總是想要我們的友誼能夠長久且持續，但是生命卻不是這樣發展的。

_____

_____

【參考答案】

In life, we all want our friendship to last long and enduring, but life just not works out that way.

③ 你可能將自己與其他人隔離開很久一段時間，而且這會對於你身體的運作有相當的損害。

_____

_____

【參考答案】

You might isolate yourself from other people for a while, and that will damage the proper function of your body.

④ 然而，時常結交新朋友，優點是你不用擔心太多，因為維持一段友誼或感情需要一個人不會給予其他人太多的壓力。

_____

_____

【參考答案】

Making new friends all the time; however, gives you the advantage of not worrying about too much since maintaining a friendship or a relationship requires a person to not give too much pressure on someone.

⑤ 如果你是個總是能夠維持一小群親密朋友的類型的人，你會時不時遭遇著像是為什麼我的普通朋友比我的親密朋友對我更好的困擾。

_____

_____

【參考答案】

If you are the type of person who always maintains a small

Part 1
獨立篇

Part 2
整合篇

number of close friends, you will encounter frustrations from time to time like why my normal friends treat me better than my close friends.

⑥ 這些疑惑和其他事情會對一個人的健康造成相當大的影響，但是如果你是個總是心態非常開放且總是交新朋友的人，你不會有這麼多的擔憂。

_____

_____

【參考答案】
These doubts and other things can be quite detrimental to one's health, but if you are the type of person who is always very open-minded and makes many new friends, you will not have a lot of worries.

⑦ 此外，他們來自於各行各業，很可能他們能充當「弱連結」的功用，替你介紹夢想工作。

_____

_____

【參考答案】
Furthermore, they are from all walks of lives, and chances are that they may act as the function of "a weak tie", introducing your dream job for you.

⑧ 你能總是獲得他們的支持，但是你卻不可能有機會像是從弱連結朋友那能帶給你的好處。

Part 1
獨立篇

Part 2
整合篇

_____

_____

【參考答案】

You can always get the support from them, but you might not even have the chance of having something that your weak ties can bring to you.

⑨「你和你的好友已經有著大多數的共同好友，你們有著重疊的社交圈」。

_____

_____

【參考答案】

"You and your best friends already know most of the same people - you have overlapping social circles".

⑩ 多數時候，我們依賴其他人介紹工作或美好的伴侶給我們。這種你知道某人，某人又知道誰的魔法會開始運作。

_____

_____

【參考答案】

Most of the time we depend on others to introduce great jobs or amazing partners to us. The you know someone who knows someone magic works.

In our life, we all expect our friendship with other people will remain, but sometimes things do not go as we expected. Some people adopt a more leisure approach by not thinking about friendship; and therefore, are more likely to retain their friendship with others. Others are fixed on maintaining friendship with a certain ritual, thinking that only by following it can friendships last and blossom. What is your opinion?

Step 1　題目中有提到對於友誼的兩種看法，先選定其中一個立場或可以像範文這樣先定義友誼，再逐步導入正題，範文指出長時間的維持一段友誼是具有報酬性的，但也會一個人造成某些程度的傷害。

Step 2　次個段落解釋會造成的負面影響。

Step 3　再來，解釋一直交新朋友的益處，例如不會有太大的壓力和比較心態等等的，並說明如此一來你可以更享受與朋友相處的時刻。

Step 4　最後提到另一件關於交新朋友的好處：你總能從不同類型

的朋友身上學習到事情。此外，還有他們能充當「弱連結」的功用。這是一個很好的闡述論點，再來進一步說明這是，一些你的親密友人無法提供的。這部分可以提升自己選擇這個論點的說服力。

※ 再來是提到暢銷書籍：「幸運如何發生」，書中探討著「與其他人的連結」。「你和你的好友已經有著大多數的共同好友，你們有著重疊的社交圈」。利用暢銷書內容更進一步強化自己的論點。

最後總結出，採取閒暇的方式是更合理的，能結交更多新朋友並創造出更多快樂。

經由先前的演練後,現在看下整篇範文並聆聽音檔。

Maintaining friendship with friends over a long period of time can be rewarding sometimes since you have a group of friends who understand you and support you along the way, but it can sometimes be quite harmful.

長時間與朋友們維持一段友誼可能有時候是具有回報的,因為你可以在一路上有一群瞭解你和支持你的朋友,但是這也可能是相當具有傷害性的。

In life, we all want our friendship to last long and enduring, but life just not works out that way. Ending a long, lasting friendship can harm a person for quite some time. You might isolate yourself from other people for a while, and that will damage the proper function of your body.

在生活中,我們總是想要我們的友誼能夠長久且持續,但是生命卻不是這樣發展的。結束一段長時間且持續的友誼可能對一個人來說傷害的時間相當長。你可能將自己與其他人隔離開很久一段時間,而且這會對於你身體的運作有相當的損害。

Making new friends all the time; however, gives you the advantage of not worrying about too much since maintaining a friendship or a relationship requires a person to not give too much pressure on someone. If you are the type of person who always maintains a small number of close friends, you will encounter frustrations from time to time like why my normal friends treat me better than my close friends. These doubts and other things can be quite detrimental to one's health, but if you are the type of person who is always very open-minded and makes many new friends, you will not have a lot of worries. You are enjoying every moment you have with your friends. The good thing is that you are not pressuring them, like pressuring them to take sides or wishing them to do things for you.

然而，時常結交新朋友，優點是你不用擔心太多，因為維持一段友誼或感情需要一個人不會給予其他人太多的壓力。一直交新朋友的話給予你不用擔心太多的優點，因為維持一段友誼或感情需要一個人不要給予其他人太多的壓力。如果你是個總是能夠維持一小群親密朋友的類型的人，你會時不時遭遇著像是為什麼我的普通朋友比我的親密朋友對我更好的困擾。這些疑惑和其他事情會對一個人的健康造成相當大的影響，但是如果你是個總是心態非常開放且總是交新朋友的人，你不會有這麼多的擔憂。你會享受著你與朋友們相處的每個時刻。好處是你不會讓他們感到壓力，會逼迫他們去選邊站或希望他們為你做什麼。

Another great thing about making new friends is that you will learn many things from different types of people. Furthermore, they are from all walks of lives, and chances are that they may act as the function of "a weak tie", introducing your dream job for you. This kind of thing is something your close friends cannot offer. Since your close friends and you form a tight circle, and it is just how the world works. You can always get the support from them, but you might not even have the chance of having something that your weak ties can bring to you.

另一件關於交新朋友的好處是，你總能從不同類型的朋友身上學習到事情。此外，他們來自於各行各業，很可能他們能充當「弱連結」的功用，替你介紹夢想工作。這些是一些你的親密友人無法提供的，因為你的親密朋友和你形成了緊密的圈子，這就是世界如何運作的。你能總是獲得他們的支持，但是你卻不可能有機會像是從弱連結朋友那能帶給你的好處。

In the book like "*How Luck Happens*", it discusses "connect to other people". "You and your best friends already know most of the same people - you have overlapping social circles". It is so true that in our life our job and love mean so much to most of us. Most of the time we depend on others to introduce great jobs or amazing partners to us. The you know someone who knows someone magic works. Lucky people are not luckier than us. They just have more new friends, so they have more opportunities. From all these reasons, I think taking a leisure approach is more reasonable and having more new friends can create more happiness because you will have the chance to get your dream job and land your potential date.

在像是在「幸運如何發生」一書中，它探討著「與其他人的連結」。「你和你的好友已經有著大多數的共同好友，你們有著重疊的社交圈」。這是如此的真實，在我們生活中我們的工作和感情是對我們大多數的人來說重要的事。多數時候，我們依賴其他人介紹工作或美好的伴侶給我們。這種你知道某人，某人又知道誰的魔法會開始運作。幸運的人並不是比我們更幸運。他們只是有著更多的新朋友，所以他們可以有更多的機會。從這些種種理由，我認為採取輕鬆的方式是更合理的，而且有更多新朋友的話能夠創造出更多快樂，因為你會有機會能獲取你的夢想工作和找到你的潛在約會對象。

UNIT 08

教育類話題⑤：主修科系的選擇和未來前途

 TASK 2 Independent Writing

Directions

Read the question below. You have 30 minutes to plan, write, and revise your essay. Typically, an effective response will contain a minimum of 300 words.

TOPIC

Traditional viewpoints have often favored students majoring in engineering and hard science over students of the humanities and social sciences, thinking that the latter has a less promising future right after students graduate from universities. Thus, people are suggesting that we should not major in History or Philosophy. What is your opinion?

整合能力強化① 實際演練 ▶ *MP3 015*

請自己動手演練並於 30 分鐘內完成至少 300 字的英文文章，盡量以
打字的方式進行，因為新托福測驗是電腦考試。

_____

_____

_____

_____

_____

_____

_____

_____

_____

_____

_____

_____

_____

_____

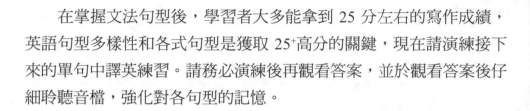

整合能力強化② 單句中譯英演練

在掌握文法句型後,學習者大多能拿到 25 分左右的寫作成績,英語句型多樣性和各式句型是獲取 25⁺高分的關鍵,現在請演練接下來的單句中譯英練習。請務必演練後再觀看答案,並於觀看答案後仔細聆聽音檔,強化對各句型的記憶。

① 歷史無疑是每個國家的基礎,而且歷史的重要性是不能被低估的。

_____

_____

【參考答案】

Without a doubt, history is the foundation for every country, and its importance cannot be downgraded.

② 在現今的社會中,許多學科都受到低估,因為父母和教育者們想要他們的孩子和下一代,在步入就業市場時,學習對他們立即有效用的事物,但是我們的社會正經歷著急遽的改變,這種改變是無法預測和難以想像的。

_____

_____

【參考答案】

In today's society, a lot of subjects are undervalued due to the fact that parents and educators want their kids and future generations to learn things that can have immediate effects when they enter the job market, but our society is undergoing a drastic change, a change that is so unpredictable and unimaginable.

③ 我們今日所認定有用的技能可能在幾年內就過時了，而且僅專注於從事特定的事情會在某些程度上危害到我們本身，而這也是我們始料未及的。

_____

_____

【參考答案】

Skills that we deem useful today can be outdated in a few years, and solely focusing on doing a certain thing can harm us in a way that we cannot imagine.

④ 主修商業的學生將重心放在如何獲取商業相關的證照或是參加與商業相關的研討會，完全沒意識到這樣雖使得他們能夠找到工作，但長遠來說對他們來說卻不是最好的。

_____

_____

【參考答案】

Students majoring in commerce will solely focus on getting the certificate related to commerce or attending seminars relevant to business, totally forgetting the fact that doing this only makes them able to find the job, but will not do them good in the long-term.

⑤ 這是她所寫道的「許多學生太專注於獲取對的分數，這樣他們才能夠進入對的學校，但如此卻使得他們無法從事些不尋常的事」。

_____

_____

【參考答案】

This is what she wrote "Many students are so focused on getting the right grades so that they can get into the right school that it barely gives them the chance to do something zany".

⑥ 她最終修習俄羅斯歷史。修俄羅斯歷史不僅使她更了解自己，也替她未來的成功鋪路。

_____

_____

【參考答案】

She eventually took Russian history. Taking Russian history not only makes her more realize herself, but also paves the path for her future success.

⑦ 她創造出幾部電影都是大熱門，因為她熟悉歷史人物。

_____

_____

【參考答案】

She created several movies that were great hits due to the fact that she knew historical figures.

⑧ 她的經驗告訴我們，我們不可能真的預測出什麼對我們來說是最有利的，而且修習歷史課碰巧在她工作中扮演了關鍵的角色。

_____

_____

【參考答案】
Her experience tells us that we cannot really predict what will benefit us and taking history classes happens to play the key role in her job.

⑨ 每個重大事件的發生或歷史人物所做的重要決定形塑著我們的思考，而且在我們有困難時給予我們所需要的智慧。

_____

_____

【參考答案】
Every major events happening or major decisions made by historical figures shapes our thinking and gives us wisdom we need at the time of the need.

Traditional viewpoints have often favored students majoring in engineering and hard science over students of the humanities and social sciences, thinking that the latter has a less promising future right after students graduate from universities. Thus, people are suggesting that we should not major in History or Philosophy. What is your opinion?

Step 1　先思考主修人文社會科學和理工科系的優缺點。主修人文社會科學像是歷史和哲學真的是錯誤的選擇嗎?

Step 2　範文首句提供了很好的定義:

※ 儘管關於選系的傳統觀點有些有事實理據,職涯軌跡並不是能預測的。

※ 人們無法很確定的表明主修某個特定的科系就意謂著你一定會比主修其他科系更成功。

※ 因此我想使用歷史作為例子,講述主修人文和社會科學也能給予你特定的優勢。

（三句話很系統且邏輯性的引入主題。）

Step 3　藉由歷史為例子，除講到優勢外，也點出因為「父母和教學家們想要他們的孩子和下一代，在步入就業市場時，學習對他們立即有效用的事物」，這根深蒂固的思考，對於孩子在選擇主修造成了影響。

Step 4　提到暢銷書 *Getting There*，以史黛西・史奈德為例子，揭露了如何免於落入該圈套和如何從研讀俄羅斯歷史最終使她功成名就的智慧。

※「許多學生太專注於獲取對的分數，這樣他們才能夠進入對的學校，但如此卻使得他們無法從事些不尋常的事」。她最終修習俄羅斯歷史。修俄羅斯歷史不僅使她更了解自己，也替了她未來的成功鋪路。

（這些都強化了文章的論點，提到人文社會科學的優勢，並解釋我們不可能預測的到學習那些事物對自己本身是最有益處的。）

Step 5　最後解釋學習歷史的好處，並總結出「我們不該受到傳統觀點而有所侷限。放寬心胸去學習所有事物，對於面對未來才是最充分的準備」。

整合能力強化④ 參考範文 ▶ *MP3 016*

經由先前的演練後，現在看下整篇範文並聆聽音檔。

Although conventional viewpoints about choosing majors have some valid facts, career trajectory cannot be predicted. People cannot be certain that having a specific major means you are bound to be successful than the others. Thus, I would love to use history as an example to illustrate that majoring in humanities and social sciences can still give you certain advantages.

儘管關於選系的傳統觀點有些有事實理據，職涯軌跡並不是能預測的。人們無法很確定的表明主修某個特定的科系就意謂著你一定會比主修其他科系更成功。因此我想使用歷史作為例子，講述主修人文和社會科學也能給予你特定的優勢。

Without a doubt, history is the foundation for every country, and its importance cannot be downgraded. In today's society, a lot of subjects are undervalued due to the fact that parents and educators want their kids and future generations to learn things that can have immediate effects when they enter the job market, but our society is undergoing a drastic change, a change that is so unpredictable and unimaginable. Skills that we deem useful today can be outdated in a few years, and solely focusing on doing a certain thing can harm us

116

in a way that we cannot imagine.

歷史無疑是每個國家的基礎，而且歷史的重要性是不能被低估的。在現今的社會中，許多學科都受到低估，因為父母和教學家們想要他們的孩子和下一代在步入就業市場時，學習對他們立即有效用的事物，但是我們的社會正經歷著急遽的改變，這種改變是無法預測和難以想像的。我們今日所認定有用的技能可能在幾年內就過時了，而且僅專注於從事特定的事情會在某些程度上危害到我們本身，而這也是我們始料未及的。

University students are now falling into that trap. Students majoring in commerce will solely focus on getting the certificate related to commerce or attending seminars relevant to business, totally forgetting the fact that doing this only makes them able to find the job, but will not do them good in the long-term.

大學學生正落入這樣的圈套。主修商業的學生將重心放在如何獲取商業相關的證照或是參加與商業相關的研討會，完全沒意識到這樣雖使得他們能夠找到工作，但長遠來說對他們來說卻不是最好的。

In "*Getting There*", one of the mentors, Stacey Snider reveals the wisdom of how to avoid the trap and how studying Russian history eventually makes who she is today. This is what she wrote "Many students are so focused on getting the right grades so that they can get into the right school that it barely gives them the chance to do something zany". She eventually took Russian history. Taking Russian history not only makes her more realize herself, but also paves the path for her future success. She created several movies that were great hits due to the fact that she knew historical figures. Her experience tells us that we cannot really predict what will benefit us and taking history classes happens to play the key role in her job. It is like Steven Jobs who does not know how handwriting will help him design iPhone.

在「勝利，並非事事順利：30 位典範人物不藏私的人生真心話」一書中，史黛西·史奈德揭露了如何免於落入該圈套和如何從研讀俄羅斯歷史最終使她功成名就的智慧。這是她所寫道的「許多學生太專注於獲取對的分數，這樣他們才能夠進入對的學校，但如此卻使得他們無法從事些不尋常的事」。她最終修習俄羅斯歷史。修俄羅斯歷史不僅使她更了解自己，也替她未來的成功鋪路。她創造出幾部電影都是大熱門，因為她熟悉歷史人物。她的經驗告訴我們，我們不可能真的預測出什麼對我們來說是最有利的，而且修習歷史課碰巧在她工作中扮演了關鍵的角色。像是賈伯斯那樣，當初也不知道手寫字對於設計iPhone 有助益。

Apart from avoiding the limitation we set on ourselves, history transcends time and place. It even crosses multiple generations. It includes two major functions: wisdom and humanity. Historical figures make us realize the wisdom from a certain person and the mind of different people. Every major events happening or major decisions made by historical figures shapes our thinking and gives us wisdom we need at the time of the need. Sometimes those things help us think about something that transcends current thinking, packaging us with greater creativity and solutions for things not yet fully understood. Sometimes it is about people. Learning personality from different historical figures smooths the frictions among people and makes us succeed, so from the above-mentioned reasons, I do think all high school graduates or university students should not be restricted to conventional views. They should be open to all fields of studies so that they can be fully prepared than those who do not.

除了能避免我們自我設限之外，歷史超越時間和地點。它甚至跨越數個世代。它包含了兩個主要功能：智慧和人性。歷史人物使得我們了解到某些特定的人的智慧和不同人的心智。每個重大事件的發生或歷史人物所做的重要決定形塑著我們的思考，而且在我們有困難時給予我們所需要的智慧。有時候那些事情幫助我們思考那些超越當今思考的事情，使我們有著更好的創造力和解決之道，對於那些尚未全然理解出頭緒的事物有更好的處理方式。有時候是關於人，學習不同歷史人物的個性，磨合人們間的摩擦會使我們成功。所以從上述的理由，我認為所有高中畢業生和大學學生都不該受到傳統觀點的侷限。他們應該對所有領域的研究都展開心胸看待，這樣他們才能比那些不放寬心者有更充分的準備。

休閒類話題①：
電視和電影
的影響

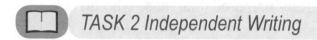

TASK 2 Independent Writing

Directions

Read the question below. You have 30 minutes to plan, write, and revise your essay. Typically, an effective response will contain a minimum of 300 words.

TOPIC

In some books, they reveal an astonishing fact that the average American spends about 9 years in their lifetime watching meaningless TVs or movies. Although it sheds some light for most of us, and watching TVs and movies does have some negative effects on our health, do viewing those have a positive influence on people? What is your opinion?

整合能力強化① 實際演練 ▶ *MP3 017*

請自己動手演練並於 30 分鐘內完成至少 300 字的英文文章，盡量以
打字的方式進行，因為新托福測驗是電腦考試。

_____

_____

_____

_____

_____

_____

_____

_____

_____

_____

_____

_____

_____

_____

_____

在掌握文法句型後，學習者大多能拿到 25 分左右的寫作成績，英語句型多樣性和各式句型是獲取 25⁺高分的關鍵，現在請演練接下來的單句中譯英練習。請務必演練後再觀看答案，並於觀看答案後仔細聆聽音檔，強化對各句型的記憶。

① 通常，我們聽到關於電影和電視對於年輕人的行為表現帶來負面影響的陳述，而即使在心底我們對於那些陳述不買單，我們已經逐漸受到那些敘述的洗腦。

　　_____

　　_____

【參考答案】
Often, we hear statements about negative effects of movies and television on the way young people behave, and even if deep down we are not buying those, we have gradually been brainwashed by those descriptions.

② 整天觀看電影和電視真的可能會導致慣於久坐的習慣，而且我們可能會成為沙發上的馬鈴薯，但是這是觀看電影和電視的極端例子。

　　_____

　　_____

【參考答案】
It is true that watching movies and television all day can lead to a

sedentary lifestyle, making us couch potatoes, but it is the extreme way of doing things.

③ 任何事情過度了都會有負面的影響，所以追根究底來說不是電影和電視本身是有害的。

_____

_____

【參考答案】

Anything that goes extreme can have harmful consequences, so it really is not movies and television themselves that are detrimental.

④ 適度的觀看電影和電視能夠提升一個人的創造力和想像力。

_____

_____

【參考答案】

Proper viewing movies and television can boost one's creativity and imagination.

⑤ 他們充當著讓我們大腦休息的短暫中途站，尤其是在工作一整天之後。

_____

_____

【參考答案】

They serve as a hiatus for our brain to take a rest, especially after a long day at work.

⑥ 我們的身體不適用於長時間的工作因為這將導致過度消耗和筋疲力竭。

_____

_____

【參考答案】
Our body is not designed to work for a significant portion of time because it will lead to burnout and exhaustion.

⑦ 觀看電影和電視使我們的大腦能從緊張的模式切換到放鬆的模式。

_____

【參考答案】
Viewing movies and television gives our brain the switch from tense modes to the relaxed mode.

⑧ 在我們觀看電影和電視的期間，我們受到有趣的電影故事情節、英俊的主角、美麗的女主角或是令人屏息的聲音效果所吸引。

_____

_____

【參考答案】
During the time we are watching them, we are leading by funny storylines, handsome actors, beautiful actresses, or breathtaking sound effects.

⑨ 當我們感到放鬆時，我們傾向放鬆。我們的身體姿勢從直立的坐姿改變成沉入沙發中。

_____

_____

【參考答案】

Our body postures change from sitting straight to sinking into the sofa. We are grabbing more cookies than we are not watching.

⑩ 此外，這是我們想出一些新奇想法或是一些我們在工作中苦思解決之道卻想不出任何計策的時候。

_____

_____

【參考答案】

In addition, this is the time we come up with some novel ideas or something that we can hardly think of when we try so hard to come up with the solution at work.

整合能力強化③ 段落拓展

In some books, they reveal an astonishing fact that the average American spends about 9 years in their lifetime watching meaningless TVs or movies. Although it sheds some light for most of us, and watching TVs and movies does have some negative effects on our health, do viewing those have a positive influence on people? What is your opinion?

Step 1　題目中提到平均每個美國人一生中花費 9 年左右的時間在看毫無意義的電視或電影上。儘管看電視或電影對於我們健康有些負面的影響，觀看電視或電影對人們有正面的影響嗎？

　　　　※ 這題只要提出自己看法並提出適切的論點去解釋即可。首段提到負面影響和洗腦，但逐步理出頭緒講明事情過猶不及，任何事太過度都會有不好的影響。

Step 2　下個段落講出適度觀看電視和電影的益處。除了提到創造力和想像力外，還提到電影和電視的目的在於讓現代人感到放鬆和調適身心。最後也表明有這樣子的壓力釋放對於一個人來說是相當重要的。

Step 3　最後一段則提到不可否認觀看電視和電影的益處，另外還提到其他方法，像是使用遙控器控制自己觀看時間，讓自己免於過度從事這項活動，從而免於負面的影響中。然後總結出自己對於這個現象的看法是正向的。

經由先前的演練後，現在看下整篇範文並聆聽音檔。

Often, we hear statements about negative effects of movies and television on the way young people behave, and even if deep down we are not buying those, we have gradually been brainwashed by those descriptions. It is true that watching movies and television all day can lead to a sedentary lifestyle, making us couch potatoes, but it is the extreme way of doing things. Anything that goes extreme can have harmful consequences, so it really is not movies and television themselves that are detrimental.

通常，我們聽到關於電影和電視對於年輕人的行為表現帶來負面影響的陳述，而即使在心底我們對於那些陳述不買單，我們已經逐漸受到那些敘述的洗腦。整天觀看電影和電視真的可能會導致久坐的習慣，而且我們可能會成為沙發上的馬鈴薯，但是這是觀看電影和電視的極端例子。任何事情過度了都會有負面的影響，所以歸根究底來說不是電影和電視本身是有害的。

Proper viewing movies and television can boost one's creativity and imagination. Movies and television are designed to make modern people relaxed. They serve as a hiatus for our brain to take a rest, especially after a long day at work. Our body is not designed to work for a significant portion of time because it will lead to burnout and exhaustion.

適度的觀看電影和電視能夠提升一個人的創造力和想像力。電影和電視的目的在於讓現代人感到放鬆。他們充當著讓我們大腦休息的短暫中途站，尤其是在工作一整天之後。我們的身體不適用於長時間的工作因為這將導致過度消耗和筋疲力竭。

Viewing movies and television gives our brain the switch from tense modes to the relaxed mode. During the time we are watching them, we are leading by funny storylines, handsome actors, beautiful actresses, or breathtaking sound effects. This is actually the time we do not have to think so hard about work or family stuff. Our stress from the day is released, and our mind becomes so peaceful. It is quite essential for anyone of us to have this kind of stress-releasing activities.

觀看電影和電視讓我們的大腦能從緊張的模式切換到放鬆的模式。在我們觀看電影和電視的期間，我們受到有趣的電影故事情節、英俊的主角、美麗的女主角或是令人屏息的聲音效果所吸引。這是我們實際上不需要思考太多關於工作和家庭事務的時候。我們一天中所受的壓力得以釋放，而且我們的心智變的很平和。有這樣子的壓力釋放活動對於我們任何一個人來說都是相當重要的。

We cannot negate the benefits of viewing movies and television. When we are relaxing, we tend to loosen up. Our body postures change from sitting straight to sinking into the sofa. We are grabbing more cookies than we are not watching.

我們不可能否認觀看電影和電視的益處。當我們感到放鬆時，我們傾向放鬆。我們的身體姿勢從直立的坐姿改變成沉入沙發中。我們比沒觀看時拿取更多的餅乾。

In addition, this is the time we come up with some novel ideas or something that we can hardly think of when we try so hard to come up with the solution at work. You just have to take the control of your time.

此外，這是我們想出一些新奇想法或是一些我們在工作中苦思解決之道卻想不出任何計策的時候。你只需要能控制好你自己的時間。

If you don't trust yourself, you can set the specific timeframe to watch movies or television, like only going to the theater to see the movies instead of sitting on the cozy bed watching movies from the Internet. Or setting the time from the remote control and only your parents know the passwords if you would like to watch more than one hour. From all these positive effects, I do think movies and television have positive effects on human beings.

如果你不信任你自己，你可以設定特定的時間來觀看電影或電視，像是只去戲院觀看電影，而非坐在舒適的床上從網路上觀看電影。如果你想要觀看多於一小時，可以在遙控器設定觀看的時間，只有你的父母知道定時的密碼。從這些正向的效果中，我認為電影和電視對於人類有著正面的影響。

UNIT 10

工作類話題③：
高薪工作、累積財富
和從事感到熱情工作的關聯性

 TASK 2 Independent Writing

Directions

Read the question below. You have 30 minutes to plan, write, and revise your essay. Typically, an effective response will contain a minimum of 300 words.

TOPIC

Some people say to accumulate wealth in shortest time, one should get a higher salary, but often a high-paid job requires you to spend much longer hours in the office. Others would rather settle down a job that requires less responsibility and workload so that they can have enough rest after a long day at work. What is your opinion?

整合能力強化① 實際演練 ▶ *MP3 019*

請自己動手演練並於 30 分鐘內完成至少 300 字的英文文章，盡量以
打字的方式進行，因為新托福測驗是電腦考試。

_____

_____

_____

_____

_____

_____

_____

_____

_____

_____

_____

_____

_____

_____

_____

_____

在掌握文法句型後，學習者大多能拿到 25 分左右的寫作成績，英語句型多樣性和各式句型是獲取 25⁺高分的關鍵，現在請演練接下來的單句中譯英練習。請務必演練後再觀看答案，並於觀看答案後仔細聆聽音檔，強化對各句型的記憶。

① 儘管人們常說「健康比財富重要」和許多其他的事情，但是在最短的時間內累積財富是能夠提早退休的方法之一。而且可能的方式就是要有較高薪資的工作。

_____

_____

【參考答案】

Although people often say "Health above wealth" and many other things, accumulating wealth in the shortest time is one of the ways to retire early and one possible way is to have a higher paid job.

② 較高薪的工作搭配著對於金錢抱有正確的心態能夠使你在生命中比其他人有更多的優勢。

_____

_____

【參考答案】

A higher paid job with the right mindset about money can give you a lot of advantages over others in life.

③ 在畢業後，他們數次嘗試從事不同的工作，這樣他們才能夠了解他們在生命中想要的是什麼。

_____

_____

【參考答案】

Right after graduation, they make several attempts to different jobs so that they can figure out what they want to do in life.

④ 比起那些準備好的人，他們遠遠落後著。這就是為什麼他們會掙扎著是否他們該從事工時較長薪資較高的工作，或是正常工時薪資普通的工作。

_____

_____

【參考答案】

Compared with those who are already prepared, they are lagging behind. That is why they arc also struggling with whether they should take a higher paid job with longer hours or an average paid job with normal work hours.

⑤ 像我這樣的人是抓住老闆給的每一次機會並且願意從事較長工時的工作。

_____

_____

【參考答案】

People like me grasp every chance given by the boss and is

135

willing to work longer hours.

⑥ 他們每日數著日子，抱怨著超時工作或是較長的工時，但是當人們找到自己有熱情的工作時，就忍受著較長工時薪資較高的工作。

_____

_____

【參考答案】

They are counting their days, fussing about working overtime or working longer hours, but people who have found their true passions can stand a higher paid job with longer hours.

⑦ 他們將自己本身的能量專注於他們設計的產品上，所以他們全然忘記的時間流逝。

_____

_____

【參考答案】

They focus so much of their energy on the product they are designing that they forget time passing by.

⑧ 這就是為什麼有句俗諺說：「當比起與朋友們相約飲酒，你對你正在從事的事情卻更感興趣時，你已經找到了你的至喜」。

_____

_____

【參考答案】

That is why there are other saying "When you are much more interested in what you're doing than going out for a drink with friends, you've found your bliss".

⑨ 還有另一句俗諺說：「目標應該要放在他人願意付你薪水去做的工作」。

_____

_____

【參考答案】

There is also another saying that "the goal should be a career in which you can't believe people actually pay you to do your job".

⑩ 當你從事你熱衷的事而且對於別人願意付你薪水做這份工作感到驚訝時，較長的工作時間似乎就不是個麻煩事或困境。

_____

_____

【參考答案】

When you are doing what you are passionate about and are surprised to find people actually pay you to do your job, working longer hours does not seem like a trouble or a dilemma.

Some people say to accumulate wealth in shortest time, one should get a higher salary, but often a high-paid job requires you to spend much longer hours in the office. Others would rather settle down a job that requires less responsibility and workload so that they can have enough rest after a long day at work. What is your opinion?

Step 1　題目中提到兩個相對的看法，各有利弊。可以從自己的工作經驗中回推，這樣會更好發揮這個題目。範文中則是選擇工時較長薪資較高的工作。手段還提到這是「在最短的時間內累積財富是能夠提早退休的方法之一」，選定了其中一個立場。

Step 2　次個段落提到了解自己的重要性，從事工作和長工時都不是重點，因為若是從事自己喜愛的工作就不會有這些顧慮。

Step 3　下個段落提到，自己明確知道自己的目標，並舉例出「不是非常了解自己的人在辦公室工作時會感到痛苦。」，更何況工時若加長。並講述「這是因為他們尚未找到自己的熱情和他們在生命中想做的事。」

之後提到找到有熱情的工作和長工時等的關聯性，最後提到暢銷書中所說的「當比起與朋友們相約飲酒，你對你正在從事的事情卻更感興趣時，你已經找到了你的至喜」，強化論點和提升說服力。

Step 4　最後一段提到，自己找到人生中的至喜，並提到另一本暢銷書中所說的：「目標應該要放在他人願意付你薪水去做的工作」，並作出進一步的推論，「當你正在從事你感到熱情的事而且對於別人願意付你薪水做這份工作時，較長的工作時間似乎就不是個麻煩事或困境」。最後總結出「基於上述提到的理由，我認為只要從事的工作是你的至喜，較長的工時不會造成困擾，而且找到一份能賦予你承擔更多責任的高薪工作，這樣一來你不會在十年後後悔自己當初並沒有真的努力過」。

（充分解釋跟推論出好幾個概念間的關聯性，且每個論點環環相扣。）

經由先前的演練後，現在看下整篇範文並聆聽音檔。

Although people often say "Health above wealth" and many other things, accumulating wealth in the shortest time is one of the ways to retire early and one possible way is to have a higher paid job. A higher paid job with the right mindset about money can give you a lot of advantages over others in life.

我會選擇工時較長薪資較高的工作。儘管人們常說「健康比財富重要」和許多其他的事情，但是在最短的時間內累積財富是能夠提早退休的方法之一，而且可能的方式就是要有較高薪資的工作。較高薪的工作搭配著對於金錢抱有正確的心態能夠使你在生命中比其他人有更多的優勢。

Nowadays people barely know themselves so they do not know what they want to do in life. Right after graduation, they make several attempts to different jobs so that they can figure out what they want to do in life. Compared with those who are already prepared, they are lagging behind. That is why they are also struggling with whether they should take a higher paid job with longer hours or an average paid job with normal work hours.

現今，人們幾乎不了解自己，所以他們不知道在生命中自己想要做什麼。在畢業後，他們數次嘗試從事不同的工作，這樣他們才能夠了解他們在生命中想要的是什麼。比起那些準備好的人，他們遠遠落後著。這就是為什麼他們會掙扎著是否他們該從事工時較長薪資較高的工作或是正常工時薪資普通的工作。

I already know what I want to do in life and which type of jobs suits me the most. People like me grasp every chance given by the boss and is willing to work longer hours. People who do not know themselves very much will feel agonized when they are in the office. This is because they have not found their passion and what they would like to do in life. They are counting their days, fussing about working overtime or working longer hours, but people who have found their true passions can stand a higher paid job with longer hours. This is not because they are workaholics. This is because they have found their passions. Time truly flies when they are in the office. They focus so much their energy on the product they are designing that they forget time passing by. That is why there are other saying "When you are much more interested in what you're doing than going out for a drink with friends, you've found your bliss".

我已經知道在生命中自己想要做什麼了，哪樣的工作最適合自己。像我這樣的人是抓住每次老闆所給的每一次機會並且願意從事較長工時的工作。不是非常了解自己的人在辦公室工作時會感到痛苦。這是因為他們尚未找到自己的熱情和他們在生命中想做的事。他們每日數著日子，抱怨著超時工作或是較長的工時，但是當人們找到自己有熱情的工作時，就能夠忍受著較長工時薪資較高的工作。這不是因為他們是工作狂。這是因為他們找到的他們的熱情。他們在辦公室裡的時間飛逝奇快。他們將自己本身的能量專注於他們設計的產品上，所以他們全然忘記了時間流逝。這就是為什麼有句俗諺說：「當比起與朋友們相約飲酒，你對你正在從事的事情卻更感興趣時，你已經找到了你的至喜」。

I am pretty lucky to say that I have found my bliss in life, so I have no problem doing a higher paid job with longer hours. There is also another saying that "the goal should be a career in which you can't believe people actually pay you to do your job". When you are doing what you are passionate about and are surprised to find people actually pay you to do your job, working longer hours does not seem like a trouble or a dilemma. When you look at your bank account, you will only feel the joy that another month passes by, and you have earned more than your co-workers and have accomplished so many things. This obviously should not be classified as a burden.

我相當幸運因為我已經找到了我人生中的至喜，所以我沒有從事工時較長薪資較高工作的問題。還有另一句俗諺說：「目標應該要放在他人願意付你薪水去做的工作」。當你從事你熱衷的事而且對於別人願意付你薪水做這份工作感到驚訝時，較長的工作時間似乎就不是個麻煩事或困境。當你看你的銀行戶頭，你只發現一個月就這麼過了，而且你已經賺的比你同事們都還多，而且你已經成就了許多事。這顯然不該被歸類成「負擔」才是。

From the above-mentioned reasons, I think working for longer hours is fine as long as it is your bliss, and find a high-paid job that shoulders your more responsibility so that you won't regret ten years later that you did not try hard enough.

基於上述提到的理由，我認為只要從事的工作是你的至喜，較長的工時不會造成困擾，而且找到一份能賦予你承擔更多責任的高薪工作，這樣一來你不會在十年後後悔自己當初並沒有真的努力過。

UNIT 11

教育類話題⑥：
孩童學習以及父母
替孩子安排過多的活動

 TASK 2 Independent Writing

Directions

Read the question below. You have 30 minutes to plan, write, and revise your essay. Typically, an effective response will contain a minimum of 300 words.

TOPIC

Today's parents arrange an endless array of activities for their kids, leaving them no room to have enough time to rest and truly engage in something they are passionate about. Kids do need time to absorb those things and learning should not be forced and arranged. It should be based on children's interest. What is your opinion?

整合能力強化① 實際演練 ▶ *MP3 021*

請自己動手演練並於 30 分鐘內完成至少 300 字的英文文章，盡量以打字的方式進行，因為新托福測驗是電腦考試。

_____

_____

_____

_____

_____

_____

_____

_____

_____

_____

_____

_____

_____

_____

_____

_____

整合能力強化② 單句中譯英演練

　　在掌握文法句型後，學習者大多能拿到 25 分左右的寫作成績，英語句型多樣性和各式句型是獲取 25⁺高分的關鍵，現在請演練接下來的單句中譯英練習。請務必演練後再觀看答案，並於觀看答案後仔細聆聽音檔，強化對各句型的記憶。

① 父母有著所有好的意圖，想要他們的孩子在起步上領先，但是這也揭露了令人擔憂的一些事情。

_____

_____

【參考答案】

Parents all have good intentions of wanting their kids to start ahead, but it also uncovers something worrisome.

② 在「你如何衡量你的人生」一書"讓你的孩子航行在賽修斯的船上"這個章節中揭露了擔憂，這能將我們導向去思考著主題，是否該給予小孩更多時間去做自己想做的事情呢？

_____

【參考答案】

In "*How Will You Measure Your Life*", the chapter of sailing your kids on Theseus's ship reveals worries that might direct us to think about the topic of whether kids should be given more time to do whatever they want.

Part 1
獨立篇

Part 2
整合篇

③ 給予小孩更多的機會去自我探索是相當值得嘉許的，但是也可能是作者所描述的「父母，通常有著心之所向，將自己本身的希望和夢想投射在自己的小孩上面」或是「當這些其他意圖不知不覺的開始作用時，父母似乎將他們的小孩導向無止盡的活動列表上，但這卻非小孩子真的有意願從事的...」。

_____

_____

【參考答案】

It's quite commendable to give children lots of opportunities to explore themselves, but it can be what the author describes "parents, often with their heart in the right place, project their own hopes and dreams onto their children" or "when these other intentions start creeping in, and parents seem to be charting their children around to an endless array of activities in which the kids are not truly engaged…".

④ 父母的投射或教師的期望可能在某種程度上傷害著小孩，讓小孩誤以為這些事情是他們應該要做的，但是數年後或是在小孩完成了某個學位後，小孩們發現自己在尷尬的處境上。

_____

_____

【參考答案】

Parents' projection or teachers' expectations can harm kids in a certain way, letting kids falsely believe it is something they should do, but years later or after kids have accomplished the degree, they find themselves in an awkward position.

⑤ 精通法律的孩子想要學習商業知識。

_____

_____

【參考答案】
Kids specialized in law want to learn business knowledge.

⑥ 此外，如果這不是小孩感到熱情的或是實際想從事的，這可能全然浪費時間和金錢。

_____

_____

【參考答案】
In addition, if it is not something kids are passionate about or truly engaged, it can be a total waste of time and money.

⑦ 安排活動應該要基於小孩的興趣，如此才能將學習的力量最大化並且有助於往後的成功。

_____

_____

【參考答案】
Arranged activities should be based on kids' interest so that it can maximize the power of learning and benefits for later success.

⑧ 回到主題上，應該給予小孩更多時間從事他們所想要做的事，因為學習不該是經由安排的。

_____

_____

【參考答案】

Back to the topic, children should be given more time to do whatever they want because learning should not be arranged.

⑨ 小孩應該要在閒暇時，發展出自己的興趣，不論是在家庭健行時對植物感到興趣，或是在海洋博物館的家庭旅遊中，想要知道更多有關於海洋生活。

_____

_____

【參考答案】

Kids should develop their own interest during leisure time whether it is about finding plants interesting during trekking with family members or it is about wanting to know more about marine life during the family trips in marine museums.

⑩ 學習應該是要自動自發的，而非強迫的。

_____

_____

【參考答案】

Learning should be spontaneous, and it should not be forced.

Today's parents arrange an endless array of activities for their kids, leaving them no room to have enough time to rest and truly engage in something they are passionate about. Kids do need time to absorb those things and learning should not be forced and arranged. It should be based on children's interest. What is your opinion?

Step 1 這題是關於子女教育的問題，題目中的敘述呈現了某一個論點，並詢問考生看法為何。若想表達的論點跟題目相同，可以延續題目中提到的論點並接續表達看法，如果有其他不同於題目敘述的想法，可以思考一下替小孩安排許多活動更多的優點等。

Step 2 首段除了先定義出「活動和這些意圖對小孩的影響」，接著使用暢銷書「你如何衡量你的人生」中的兩個具體舉例：

※ 「父母，通常有著心之所向，將自己本身的希望和夢想投射在自己的小孩上面」。

※ 「當這些其他意圖不知不覺的開始作用時，父母似乎將他們的小孩導向無止盡的活動列表上，但這卻非小孩子

真的有意願從事的...」。

這兩句都闡述了父母對小孩造成了影響，並且留了許多可以討論的空間，這些影響都使得我們去思考題目所說的「安排活動」，這是父母加在小孩身上的，下段可以再藉由這部分的重點作進一步的論述。

Step 3　這段延續講述父母的投射和教師的期望，並指出如果這些活動和過程中儘管學習的項目頗多，但是若非小孩子本身感到熱情或想從事的，最終對小孩子並不是最好的。

Step 4　緊接著拉回主題上，應該讓小孩作自我探索並找到興趣，並指出「學習應該是要逐步發展的而且是由內部驅策的。」。

Step 5　最後呼應題目敘述，講述大腦確實需要時間去吸收新知，孩子才能快樂並在學習中實現自我。

經由先前的演練後，現在看下整篇範文並聆聽音檔。

It is true that nowadays kids spend more time on doing lots of activities whether it is the activity assigned by the school or the activity deliberately arranged by some parents. Parents all have good intentions of wanting their kids to start ahead, but it also uncovers something worrisome.

現今小孩真的花費更多時間從事許多活動，不論活動是否由學校所指定的或是有些父母刻意安排的。父母有著所有好的意圖，想要他們的孩子在起步上領先，但是這也揭露了令人擔憂的一些事情。

In *"How Will You Measure Your Life"*, the chapter of sailing your kids on Theseus's ship reveals worries that might direct us to think about the topic of whether kids should be given more time to do whatever they want. It's quite commendable to give children lots of opportunities to explore themselves, but it can be what the author describes "parents, often with their heart in the right place, project their own hopes and dreams onto their children" or "when these other intentions start creeping in, and parents seem to be charting their children around to an endless array of activities in which the kids are not truly engaged⋯".

Part 1
獨立篇

Part 2
整合篇

在「你如何衡量你的人生」一書"讓你的孩子航行在賽修斯的船上"這個章節中揭露了擔憂，這能將我們導向去思考著主題，是否該給予小孩更多時間去做自己想做的事情呢？給予小孩更多的機會去自我探索是相當值得嘉許的，但是也可能是作者所描述的「父母，通常有著心之所向，將自己本身的希望和夢想投射在自己的小孩上面」或是「當這些其他意圖不知不覺的開始作用時，父母似乎將他們的小孩導向無止盡的活動列表上，但這卻非小孩子真的有意願從事的…」。

Parents' projection or teachers' expectations can harm kids in a certain way, letting kids falsely believe it is something they should do, but years later or after kids have accomplished the degree, they find themselves in an awkward position. Kids specialized in law want to learn business knowledge. In addition, if it is not something kids are passionate about or truly engaged, it can be a total waste of time and money. Arranged activities should be based on kids' interest so that it can maximize the power of learning and benefits for later success.

父母的投射或教師的期望可能在某種程度上傷害著小孩，讓小孩誤以為這些事情是他們應該要做的，但是數年後或是在小孩完成了某個學位後，小孩們發現自己在尷尬的處境上。精通法律的孩子想要學習商業知識。此外，如果這不是小孩感到熱情的或是實際想從事的，這可能全然浪費時間和金錢。安排活動應該要基於小孩的興趣，如此才能將學習的力量最大化並且有助益於往後的成功。

Back to the topic, I think children should be given more time to do whatever they want because learning should not be arranged. It should be developed. Kids should develop their own interest during leisure time whether it is about finding plants interesting during trekking with family members or it is about wanting to know more about marine life during the family trips in marine museums. Learning should be spontaneous, and it should not be forced. It should be gradually developed and internally motivated.

回到主題上，我認為應該給予小孩更多時間從事他們所想要做的事，因為學習不該是經由安排的。學習應該是由發展而來的。小孩應該要在閒暇時，發展出自己的興趣，不論是在家庭健行時對植物感到興趣，或是在海洋博物館的家庭旅遊中，想要知道更多有關於海洋生活。學習應該是要自動自發的，而非強迫的。學習應該是要逐步發展的而且是由內部驅策的。

Our brain does need time to rest and consume knowledge. Only by giving them flexible time to explore what they are truly passionate about and absorb what they have learned during those activities and later focus your sole attention on assisting your kids to achieve their short-term and long-term goals can they have a happier and more fulfilling life.

我們的大腦確實是需要時間休息和吸收知識。只有給予孩子們彈性的時間去探索自我，找到真的感到熱忱的事物和吸收他們在那些活動中所學到的，並於稍後將你的重心僅放在協助孩子們達到他們短期和長期目標，這樣他們才能夠有更快樂且實現自我的生活。

UNIT 12

一般話題①：
具經驗和專業人士

 TASK 2 Independent Writing

Directions

Read the question below. You have 30 minutes to plan, write, and revise your essay. Typically, an effective response will contain a minimum of 300 words.

TOPIC

"Experienced" is a too powerful word used by modern people. Most people are led to believed that experienced professionals, such as doctors and attorneys, perform relatively well than young professionals because they have more experience. What's your opinion?

整合能力強化① 實際演練 ▶ *MP3 023*

請自己動手演練並於 30 分鐘內完成至少 300 字的英文文章，盡量以
打字的方式進行，因為新托福測驗是電腦考試。

整合能力強化② 單句中譯英演練

　　在掌握文法句型後，學習者大多能拿到 25 分左右的寫作成績，英語句型多樣性和各式句型是獲取 25⁺高分的關鍵，現在請演練接下來的單句中譯英練習。請務必演練後再觀看答案，並於觀看答案後仔細聆聽音檔，強化對各句型的記憶。

① 他們誤以為較大型的醫院比起小型醫院更好，這樣他們才能受到更多的醫療治療和照護。

_____

_____

【參考答案】

They have been misled into believing that bigger hospitals are better than the small ones so that they can get better medication and care.

② 有些人甚至在網路上做了更小心翼翼的功課，比較著醫生名單，確保他們可以獲得最佳的照護。

_____

_____

【參考答案】

Some people even do meticulous work by comparing the list of doctors online to ensure they can get the best care possible.

③ 誤解迴盪在人們心中，而且誤解很難從人們心中剃除。

_____

_____

【參考答案】

Misconceptions linger in people's mind, and they have become so hard to get rid of.

④ 儘管許多看似合理的言論蔓延在雙方立場上，專家的觀點值得我們去探討，我們也能從中得到較合理的結論。

_____

_____

【參考答案】

Although lots of seemingly plausible arguments rampant among both sides, it is quite worthwhile to take a look at what experts have to say about this phenomenon so that we can reach a sounder conclusion about it.

⑤ 在「刻意練習：來自新科學專業」一書中，它揭露了關於學習上驚人的事實，而且「在這個評論中﹨的六十個研究中幾乎都顯示，醫生的表現隨著時間而呈現更糟的情況或維持不變」。

_____

_____

【參考答案】

In "*Peak, Secrets from the New Science of Expertise*", it reveals astonishing facts about learning, and "In almost every one of the five dozen studies included in the review, doctors' performance grew worse over time or stayed about the same".

⑥ 「年資較深的醫生所知道的較少而且在提供適當照護上，比起僅有較少年資經驗的醫生表現的更差」。

_____

_____

【參考答案】

"The older doctors knew less and did worse in terms of providing appropriate care than doctors with far fewer years of experience."

⑦ 「如果持續教育沒有使得醫生有效的精進，那麼隨著年資增長，他們的技能就更落後於現今的技術」。

_____

_____

【參考答案】

"if continuing education does not keep doctors effectively updated, then the older they get, the less current their skill will be".

⑧ 如果事情是這樣的話，那麼具經驗的醫生應該要持續學習新的東西，這樣他們才能夠在表現上超越年輕醫生。

_____

_____

【參考答案】

If this is the case, then experienced doctors should continue learning new things so that they can still outperform young doctors.

⑨ 並不是說具經驗的醫生不是細心的醫生，但是他們傾向認為有些程序他們做過上百次了，所以他們沒有像年輕醫生那樣小心翼翼，認為自己不具經驗，所以更該花費更多額外的心力在每個步驟上。

_____

_____

【參考答案】

It is not that experienced doctors are not careful doctors, but they tend to think some procedures as something that they have done thcm a hundred times, so they are not as careful as young doctors, who are inexperienced so that they put extra attention to every step.

⑩ 要記住的是錯誤就是錯誤，而且一個錯誤可能導致令人感到遺憾的傷害。這些小事情像是投入更多額外的照護或是注意力都可能實際上補足醫療經驗的不足。

_____

_____

【參考答案】

Keep in mind that an error is an error, and an error can result in regrettable harm. Those little things like putting extra care or attention can actually make up for a lack of experience.

"Experienced" is a too powerful word used by modern people. Most people are led to believed that experienced professionals, such as doctors and attorneys, perform relatively well than young professionals because they have more experience. What's your opinion?

Step 1　這題提到經驗還有傳統的刻板印象,以至於大家會認為具專業經驗者比年輕的專業人士表現得更好。

Step 2　這題蠻難發揮的,而段落首句先以鋪陳的部分講述並反問真的是如此嗎,接著以其中一個行業,醫生的部分為例去討論。

Step 3　提到大家對於大醫院和小醫院的錯誤認知,並指出這些「誤解迴盪在人們心中,而且誤解很難從人們心中剃除。」,最後拉回這個主題。

Step 4　使用暢銷書「刻意練習:來自新科學專業」具體解釋
　　　　　※「在這個評論的六十個研究中幾乎都顯示,醫生的表現隨著時間而呈現更糟的情況或維持不變」。
　　　　　※「年資較深的醫生所知道的較少而且在提供適當照護

上，比起僅有較少年資經驗的醫生表現的更差」。

（這兩句能強化表達，比起僅一般性論述但講不出所以然或很 general 的文法正確文句有效多了）。

Step 5　最後一段更進一步講述「持續的教育是關鍵。」

※「如果持續教育沒有使得醫生有效的精進，那麼隨著年資增長，他們的技能就會落後於現今的技術。」

除了講述持續學習，也講到另外幾項重點：

※ 世界是變化的如此快速。

※「具有經驗對一個人來說也可能是巨大的阻撓」，因為他們會有著「我知道自己在做什麼」的觀念存在。

※ 耐心和細心也扮演著關鍵角色。

※ 年輕醫生認為自己不具經驗，所以花費更多額外的心力在每個步驟上。

最後綜合這些因素後作出總結。

經由先前的演練後,現在看下整篇範文並聆聽音檔。

It's true that "experienced" means a lot to many people, and it's like a gilded title. People are buying the word "experienced", but do experienced professionals always perform well than younger professionals? I would like to use doctors as an example to discuss this phenomenon.

對許多人來說,「具經驗的」意義重大,這就像是個鍍金的頭銜。人們會因為「具經驗的」而買單,但是具經驗的專業人士總是表現得比年輕的專業人士佳嗎?我想要用醫生這個行業為例子來討論這個現象。

Whenever people are getting sick, the first thing that pops into their mind is to go to the hospital, preferably the bigger one. They have been misled into believing that bigger hospitals are better than the small ones so that they can get better medication and care. Some people even do meticulous work by comparing the list of doctors online to ensure they can get the best care possible. Misconceptions linger in people's mind, and they have become so hard to get rid of. Sometimes it will lead to a fight between whether bigger hospitals are obviously better or experienced doctors are better than young doctors. These all lead to today's topic of whether experienced professionals are better than young professionals.

每當人們生病時，在他們心中首先想到的是事情是去醫院，且偏好較大型的醫院。他們誤以為較大型的醫院比起小型醫院更好，這樣他們才能受到更多的醫療治療和照護。有些人甚至在網路上做了更小心翼翼的功課，比較著醫生名單，確保他們可以獲得最佳的照護。誤解迴盪在人們心中，而且誤解很難從人們心中刪除。有時候這導致了爭吵，關於較大型的醫院顯然較好或是具經驗的醫生比起年輕醫生來說更好。這些都導向今天的主題，是否具有經驗的專業人士比起較年輕的專業人士來說更好。

Although lots of seemingly plausible arguments rampant among both sides, it is quite worthwhile to take a look at what experts have to say about this phenomenon so that we can reach a sounder conclusion about it. In *"Peak, Secrets from the New Science of Expertise"*, it reveals astonishing facts about learning, and "In almost every one of the five dozen studies included in the review, doctors' performance grew worse over time or stayed about the same". "The older doctors knew less and did worse in terms of providing appropriate care than doctors with far fewer years of experience."

儘管許多看似合理的言論蔓延在雙方立場上，專家的觀點相當值得我們去探討，我們也能從中得到較合理的結論。在「刻意練習：來自新科學專業」一書中，它揭露了關於學習上驚人的事實，而且「在評論的六十個研究中幾乎都顯示，醫生的表現隨著時間而呈現更糟的情況或維持不變」。「年資較深的醫生所知道的較少而且在提供適當照護上，比起僅有較少年資經驗的醫生表現的更差」。

This is pretty contrary to what people think about experienced doctors. In addition, continual education is the key. "if continuing education does not keep doctors effectively updated, then the older they get, the less current their skill will be". This applies to every profession because the world is changing so fast. New skills will become obsolete in such a short time. If this is the case, then experienced doctors should continue learning new things so that they can still outperform young doctors.

這與人們對於具經驗的醫生所了解的全然不同。此外，持續的教育是關鍵。「如果持續教育沒有使得醫生有效的精進，那麼隨著年資增長，他們的技能就會落後於現今的技術」。這能應用於每個職業中，因為世界是變化的如此快速。新技能可能在短時間內就過時了。如果事情是這樣的話，那麼具經驗的醫生應該要持續學習新的東西，這樣他們才能夠在表現上超越年輕醫生。

Also, they should stay humble. Experienced can be a great hindrance for a person since they have the mindset of "I know what I am doing". Patience and carefulness are also the key. It is not that experienced doctors are not careful doctors, but they tend to think some procedures as something that they have done them a hundred times, so they are not as careful as young doctors, who are inexperienced so that they put extra attention to every step. Keep in mind that an error is an error, and an error can result in regrettable harm. Those little things like putting extra care or attention can actually make up for a lack of experience. To sum up, with all reasons mentioned above, I do not agree that experienced professionals are better than young professionals.

而且，他們應該要保持謙虛。具有經驗對一個人來說也可能是巨大的阻撓，因為他們會有著「我知道自己在做什麼」的觀念存在。耐心和細心也扮演著關鍵角色。並不是說具經驗的醫生不是細心的醫生，但是他們傾向認為有些程序他們他們做過上百次了，所以他們沒有像年輕醫生那樣小心翼翼，認為自己不具經驗，所以更該花費更多額外的心力在每個步驟上。要記住的是錯誤就是錯誤，而且一個錯誤可能導致令人感到遺憾的傷害。這些小事情像是投入更多額外的照護或是注意力都可能實際上補足醫療經驗的不足。總之，基於上述這些所有理由，我不同意具經驗的專業人士比起年輕的專業人士表現更好。

UNIT 13

一般類話題②：
寵物在愛好寵物者
心中的位置

 TASK 2 Independent Writing

Directions

Read the question below. You have 30 minutes to plan, write, and revise your essay. Typically, an effective response will contain a minimum of 300 words.

TOPIC

People in some nations are eating or used to eat pets, such as dogs and cats, but nowadays people's attitude toward pets have changed. People now adore their pets and are even willing to spend a great deal of money on them. Some people think this kind of behavior is a bit too much because they are just pets, not children. What is your opinion?

整合能力強化① 實際演練 ▶ *MP3 025*

請自己動手演練並於 30 分鐘內完成至少 300 字的英文文章，盡量以打字的方式進行，因為新托福測驗是電腦考試。

_____

_____

_____

_____

_____

_____

_____

_____

_____

_____

_____

_____

_____

_____

_____

_____

整合能力強化② 單句中譯英演練

　　在掌握文法句型後，學習者大多能拿到 25 分左右的寫作成績，英語句型多樣性和各式句型是獲取 25⁺高分的關鍵，現在請演練接下來的單句中譯英練習。請務必演練後再觀看答案，並於觀看答案後仔細聆聽音檔，強化對各句型的記憶。

① 從新聞標題中，我們通常可以發現一些惱人的事情，像是小孩子遺棄他們的父母或是一個男人對他的妻子不忠，而當然這個清單可以無限延伸下去。

　　_____

　　_____

【參考答案】
From news headlines, we can often find something upsetting like kids abandoning their parents or a guy who cheated on his wife, and of course the list can go on and on.

② 重點是即使我們應該要對人感到信賴而且有個好心腸，但是信賴是受到高估的。

　　_____

　　_____

【參考答案】
The point is even if we should trust people and have a good heart, but trust is overrated.

③ 事情總是能在轉眼間產生變化，不論是對於聖誕節派對的裝飾或是事情不照你的方式走之類的意見不合。

_____

_____

【參考答案】

Things can always change in the blink of an eye whether it is the disagreement about the decorations over the Christmas party or things just do not go your way.

④ 寵物總是待在我們身旁陪伴著我們。他們不會對你不忠。在正常情況下，寵物不會離開你。

_____

_____

【參考答案】

Pets are always there for us. They cannot cheat on you. Under normal circumstances, they will not leave you.

⑤ 不論是你正苦惱著關於離婚的事或者是在電話中宣洩對鄰居的不滿，寵物總是聆聽著，或是寵物假裝著牠們有在聽你講話。

_____

_____

【參考答案】

Whether you are upsetting about the divorce or venting over the phone about your neighbors, they always listen, or they pretend they are listening to you.

⑥ 有了這樣的認知後，我想人們就不會對於為什麼養寵物的人會花費那麼多金錢寵牠們有異議，這是相當能理解的。

_____

_____

【參考答案】

With this kind of understanding, I think people will not have another opinion about why people with pets spend so much money adoring them, and it is perfectly understandable.

⑦ 在經歷了人生的起起伏伏後，寵物可能僅是所剩餘的陪伴者。

_____

_____

【參考答案】

After experiencing life's ups and downs, they are probably the ones left.

⑧ 此外，關於有更佳的使用金錢方式的陳述，似乎像是對那些喜愛寵物或是養寵物者的偏見。

_____

_____

【參考答案】

In addition, the statements of there are better uses for this money seem like prejudices against someone who love pets or raise pets.

172

⑨ 有些人將他們的昂貴車當作了他們的妻子，而且他們不介意花費
許多錢維持車的外觀，即使他們早知道車的價值會在你購買後大
幅降低。

_____

_____

【參考答案】
Some people think of their expensive cars as their wives, and they
do not mind spending so much money maintaining the look, even
though they know too well that the value of cars dwindles
significantly right after your purchase.

⑩ 如果你可以將這部分詮釋成你的朋友只是想要寵寵他們的兒子，
你就不會有這樣子的看法，就像是當你想要讓你的小孩快樂，就
不會認為這些花費太驚人，因為你會珍惜這樣的時刻。

_____

_____

【參考答案】
If you can interpret it in a way that your friend just wants to adore
their sons, you will not have this kind of opinion, just like you
will not think it costs so much, if you want to make your kids
happy and you cherish this moment.

People in some nations are eating or used to eat pets, such as dogs and cats, but nowadays people's attitude toward pets have changed. People now adore their pets and are even willing to spend a great deal of money on them. Some people think this kind of behavior is a bit too much because they are just pets, not children. What is your opinion?

Step 1　題目是關於人們和寵物間的關係，其實人們對寵物的態度已經有很大的改變，範文中是贊同將寵物視為自己的小孩或親密朋友，並藉由論述說明寵自己的寵物是合理的。

Step 2　首段使用較不一樣的手法開始描述，以新聞標題等作為切入點，逐步講到寵物的忠心和他們受喜愛的原因。這些原因都促成大家會寵愛寵物的原因。

Step 3　第二段更提到寵物是 listeners，這使得寵物並非評論者所看到的部份，喜愛寵物者的認知是「寵物應該要被歸類在家庭成員類別裡。」。

Step 4　次個段落講述有了這樣的認知後，就能理解花費許多金錢在寵物身上的人為什麼會有這樣的行為，最後指出只是人

們所重視的東西不同而已。

Step 5　在前面幾個段落的逐步且環環相扣的論述後，最後一段以汽車為例子，最後拉回寵物身上並寫道人們該尊重這樣的行為。

Part 1
獨立篇

Part 2
整合篇

經由先前的演練後,現在看下整篇範文並聆聽音檔。

From news headlines, we can often find something upsetting like kids abandoning their parents or a guy who cheated on his wife, and of course the list can go on and on. The point is even if we should trust people and have a good heart, trust is overrated. Things can always change in the blink of an eye whether it is the disagreement about the decorations over the Christmas party or things just do not go your way. Human beings can always change, but not pets. Pets are always there for us. They cannot cheat on you. Under normal circumstances, they will not leave you.

從新聞標題中,我們通常可以發現一些惱人的事情,像是小孩子遺棄他們的父母或是一個男人對他的妻子不忠,而當然這個清單可以無限延伸下去。重點是即使我們應該要對人感到信賴而且有個好心腸,但是信賴是受到高估的。事情總是能在轉眼間產生變化,不論是對於聖誕節派對的裝飾或是事情不照你的方式走之類的意見不合。人類總是會改變,但是寵物卻不會。寵物總是待在我們身旁陪伴著我們。他們不會對你不忠。在正常情況下,寵物不會離開你。

Of course, you have to treat them well. They will always be there for you when you come home. Whether you are upsetting about the divorce or venting over the phone about your neighbors, they always listen, or they pretend they are listening to you. People start to have a different feeling toward their pet. People think of them as their sons, daughters, or close friends. To people who raise pets, pets should not be narrowly classified as pets. They should be classified as family members.

當然，你必須要善待他們。他們總是會陪伴著你，當你回到家時。不論是你正苦惱著關於離婚的事或者是在電話中宣洩對鄰居的不滿，寵物總是聆聽著，或是寵物假裝著牠們有在聽你講話。人們開始對於牠們的寵物有著不同的感受。他們將他們的寵物當成了兒子、女兒或是親密朋友。對於眷養寵物的人來說，寵物不應該被侷限在寵物的範疇。寵物應該被視為「家庭成員」。

With this kind of understanding, I think people will not have another opinion about why people with pets spend so much money adoring them, and it is perfectly understandable. People need someone they can count on. After experiencing life's ups and downs, they are probably the ones left.

有了這樣的認知後，我想人們就不會對於為什麼養寵物的人會花費那麼多金錢寵牠們有異議，這是相當能理解的。人需要有他們所能依賴的伴。在經歷了人生的起起伏伏後，寵物可能僅是所剩餘的陪伴者。

In addition, the statements of there are better uses for this money seem like prejudices against someone who love pets or raise pets. After all it is their money. In life, people value different things.

此外，關於有更佳的使用金錢方式的陳述，似乎像對那些喜愛寵物或是養寵物者的偏見。畢竟，這也是他們的錢。在生活中，人們重視的東西不同。

Some people think of their expensive cars as their wives, and they do not mind spending so much money maintaining the look, even though they know too well that the value of cars dwindles significantly right after your purchase. The same holds true for people who love pets. "Better uses for this money" is so weird in this situation. The value of the money should be spent on purchasing which things is not something for us to decide, it lies in the person who makes use of them. If you can interpret it in a way that your friend just wants to adore their sons, you will not have this kind of opinion, just like you will not think it costs so much, if you want to make your kids happy and you cherish this moment.

有些人將他們昂貴的車當作他們的妻子，而且他們不介意花費許多錢維持車的外觀，即使他們早知道車的價值會在你購買後大幅降低。這道理適用於喜歡寵物的人。「更佳的使用此金錢」在這個情況下是很奇怪的。金錢的價值應該花費在哪些事物上，不是由我們來決定的，而是使用金錢的人。如果你可以將這部分詮釋成你的朋友只是想要寵寵他們的兒子，你就不會有這樣子的看法，就像是當你想要讓你的小孩快樂，就不會認為這些花費太驚人，因為你會珍惜這樣的時刻。

Therefore, I do think it is pretty reasonable that people would like to pamper their pets or treat them like their own kids. People should respect the way they spend a great deal of money on their pets.

因此，我認為人們想要寵愛他們的寵物或把他們視為己出是相當合理的。人們應該要尊重他們在寵物身上花大把鈔票的行為。

UNIT 14

教育類話題⑦：
數位時代令孩子分心的
事物導致父母教育上的困難

 TASK 2 Independent Writing

Directions

Read the question below. You have 30 minutes to plan, write, and revise your essay. Typically, an effective response will contain a minimum of 300 words.

TOPIC

Today's kids are having more distractions in life. Distractions, such as smartphones, are one of the main reasons that they underperform in the school setting. Some people claim that those distractions are making raising kids so hard nowadays because they even bring the safety issue of their kids to the table, and this is something much more important than getting a good grade. What is your opinion?

整合能力強化① 實際演練 ▶ *MP3 027*

請自己動手演練並於 30 分鐘內完成至少 300 字的英文文章，盡量以打字的方式進行，因為新托福測驗是電腦考試。

_____

_____

_____

_____

_____

_____

_____

_____

_____

_____

_____

_____

_____

整合能力強化② 單句中譯英演練

　　在掌握文法句型後，學習者大多能拿到 25 分左右的寫作成績，英語句型多樣性和各式句型是獲取 25⁺高分的關鍵，現在請演練接下來的單句中譯英練習。請務必演練後再觀看答案，並於觀看答案後仔細聆聽音檔，強化對各句型的記憶。

① 在過去，沒有數位裝置，父母沒什麼好擔心的，或許唯一需要擔憂的是他們的小孩是否在外頭玩耍時受傷了。

_____

_____

【參考答案】

In the past, without digital devices, parents had nothing to worry about, and perhaps the only concern was whether their kids would get injured while they were playing outside.

② 現今，數位裝置蔓延著而且無所不在，這使得相關的安全議題浮上檯面，因為大多數的危害是隱形的。

_____

_____

【參考答案】

Nowadays, digital devices are rampant and everywhere, and they bring the safety issue to the table, since most of the harm is invisible.

③ 即使父母想要保護他們的小孩，父母發現自己對於小孩們全然毫無頭緒，像是他們在臉書或其他社群網站上與誰交談。

【參考答案】
Even if parents want to protect their kids, they find themselves completely clueless about their kids, like whom are they talking to on Facebook or other networking sites.

④ 父母勉為其難地相信他們的十歲女兒在午夜跟一個全然的陌生人見面，直到他們在住家附近目睹了此刻。

【參考答案】
Parents are reluctantly believing that their ten-year-old daughter will go out with a complete stranger in the midnight until they are witnessing the moment near the place they live.

⑤ 這真的使得現今養育孩子比起過去更艱難，因為父母不可能總是追蹤小孩子的蹤跡，甚至在小孩子睡覺時。

【參考答案】
This really makes educating kids more difficult than raising kids in the past since parents cannot always track down their kids'

whereabouts even during the time they are sleeping.

⑥ 甚至是成年人都無可避免潛藏在那些社交網站下的危險。

_____

_____

【參考答案】
Even grown-ups cannot be immune from the danger lurking beneath those networking sites.

⑦ 這顯然對於今日的父母亮起了紅旗，因為他們無法不去控制自己的小孩。

_____

_____

【參考答案】
This clearly raises the red flag for today's parents that they cannot let go the control of their kids.

⑧ 有些小孩甚至使用父母的信用卡去購買虛擬世界的武器因為小孩想要讓他們的遊戲角色更強大。

_____

_____

【參考答案】
Some even use parents' credit cards to buy weapons in the virtual world because kids want their characters more powerful.

⑨ 小孩就像是病毒般，不斷地演化出新的形式，而父母過於疲憊而無法應付。

_____

_____

【參考答案】

Kids are like viruses, constantly evolving into a new form, and parents are too tired to combat.

⑩ 現今的小孩的價值觀受到 iPhone 和許多昂貴的物品所影響而加劇崩壞，而且他們不會珍惜東西。

_____

_____

【參考答案】

Today's kids' value is aggravated by iPhones and lots of expensive stuff and they do not cherish things.

Today's kids are having more distractions in life. Distractions, such as smartphones, are one of the main reasons that they underperform in the school setting. Some people claim that those distractions are making raising kids so hard nowadays because they even bring the safety issue of their kids to the table, and this is something much more important than getting a good grade. What is your opinion?

Step 1　這題主要是關於 distractions in life 對小孩身心健康等許多層面造成的影響，而比起在學校考試拿到高分，孩子的安全可能是更重要的。

Step 2　首段先使用了對比的方式，對照出在過去沒有數位裝置和現在生活中有的數位裝置的差異。

Step 3　次段舉例了電視節目的例子，這使得家長開始需要擔心這些數位裝置所產生的後續影響。段落中更舉例了這些潛藏的危險導致的社會事件。

Step 4　下個段落講到線上遊戲，這也是導致孩子在學習上分心和與父母衝突的點。也提到了小孩子價值觀的扭曲和小孩子不懂得珍惜生活中的事物。

Step 5　最後總結出「所有這些令人分心的事物，例如智慧型手機、線上遊戲和社群網站，使孩子們分心而無法表現正常等等」，還有父母該更費心於讓小孩子免於受到這些事物的影響。

Part 1
獨立篇

Part 2
整合篇

經由先前的演練後,現在看下整篇範文並聆聽音檔。

In the past, without digital devices, parents had nothing to worry about, and perhaps the only concern was whether their kids would get injured while they were playing outside. Parents' usual conversations with their kids would be go play outside. Nowadays, digital devices are rampant and everywhere, and they bring the safety issue to the table, since most of the harm is invisible. Even if parents want to protect their kids, they find themselves completely clueless about their kids, like whom are they talking to on Facebook or other networking sites.

在過去,沒有數位裝置,父母沒什麼好擔心的,或許唯一需要擔憂的是他們的小孩是否在外頭玩耍時受傷了。父母與子女間慣有對話是去外頭玩耍吧。現今,數位裝置蔓延著而且無所不在,這使得相關的安全議題浮上檯面,因為大多數的危害是隱形的。即使父母想要保護他們的小孩,父母發現自己對於小孩們全然毫無頭緒,像是他們在臉書或其他社群網站上與誰交談。

Parents are reluctantly believing that their ten-year-old daughter will go out with a complete stranger in the midnight until they are witnessing the moment near the place they live. They find themselves lucky because it is the setup by a TV program to let parents be more aware of the danger lurking beneath the social networking site. This really makes educating kids more difficult than raising kids in the past since parents cannot always track down their kids' whereabouts even during the time they are sleeping.

父母勉為其難地相信他們的十歲女兒在午夜跟一個全然的陌生人見面，直到他們在住家附近目睹了此刻。父母覺得出自己挺幸運，因為這是電視節目的安排，讓父母更警覺潛藏在社群網站內的危險。這真的使得現今養育孩子比起過去更艱難，因為父母不可能總是追蹤小孩子的蹤跡，甚至在小孩子睡覺時。

Recently, astounding news shocked most of parents. Even grown-ups cannot be immune from the danger lurking beneath those networking sites. First a female was murdered by her boyfriend whom she met on-line. Then a 30-year-old grown-up was murdered by a guy whom she would not want to have sex with. This clearly raises the red flag for today's parents that they cannot let go the control of their kids. Dangers are everywhere.

近期，驚人的新聞嚇到了大多數的父母。甚至是成年人都無可避免潛藏在那些社交網站下的危險。首先是位女性受到她在網路上認識的男友殺害。然後是位三十歲得成年女性被一位她不願意與之發生性關係的男子殺害。這顯然對於今日的父母亮起了紅旗，因為他們無法不去控制自己的小孩。危險無所不在。

Another thing parents should be worried about is online games. Kids can become so addicted to the game that their personality becomes so eccentric. Some even use parents' credit cards to buy weapons in the virtual world because kids want their characters to be more powerful. Others have aggressive behaviors toward friends who play better than they.

另一件事父母需要擔心的是線上遊戲。小孩會變得沉迷遊戲，以至於他們的個性變得相當古怪。有些小孩甚至使用父母的信用卡去購買虛擬世界的武器因為小孩想要讓他們的遊戲角色更強大。其他人對於遊戲中玩得比他們好的朋友則有著攻擊性的行為。

All these modern-day phenomena make parents tiresome. Kids are like viruses, constantly evolving into a new form, and parents are too tired to combat. One kid even went to the extreme, destroying all furniture at home simply because their parents will not let him buy the new iPhone. His iPhone is not even a half year old. Today's kids' value is aggravated by iPhones and lots of expensive stuff and they do not cherish things. They do not know money is not easily earned.

所有這些現代的現象都使得父母感到疲憊。小孩就像是病毒般，不斷地演化出新的形式，而父母則過於疲憊而無法應付。有位小孩甚至表現得極端，毀壞家裡的所有傢俱僅因為他的父母不讓他購買新的 iPhone。他的 iPhone 甚至才使用不到半年。現今的小孩的價值觀受到 iPhone 和許多昂貴的物品的影響而加劇崩壞，而且他們不會珍惜東西。他們不知道金錢取之不易。

All these distractions, such as smartphones, online games, and social networking sites, are diverting kids from performing normal, let alone getting a good grade. Perhaps today's parents should work really hard to reduce or remove those distractions so that their own kids can perform well in the school setting and be safe all the time.

所有這些令人分心的事物，例如智慧型手機、線上遊戲和社群網站，使孩子們分心而無法表現正常，更別說是要獲取高分了。或許現今的父母應該要花費更多努力降低或移除這些分心的事物，這樣他們的孩子們才能在學校環境中表現良好而且一直都處於安全情況下。

Part 2 整合篇

整合篇的話則包含需要閱讀一小段文章和聽一段講座或敘述，整合聽和讀的訊息後，再將重點呈現出。在這部分，聽力內容扮演彎關鍵的部分，要多留心聽力內容並比較與閱讀內容的相似或差異處。

此外，書籍中規劃了口譯單句中譯英，可以藉由練習這部分加強口說和寫作整合答題能力，如果想提升整合篇的熟練度，可以藉由多寫TPO試題強化答題的熟練度。

UNIT
01

美國教育類：
中文學習潮

The Chinese Learning Craze in the U.S.

 INSTRUCTIONS

You have **20 minutes** to plan and write your response. Your response will be judged on the basis of the quality of your writing and on how well your response presents the points in the lecture and their relationships to the reading passage. Typically, an effective response will be 150 to 225 words.

Summarize the points made in the lecture you just heard, explaining how they cast doubt on points made in the reading.

Reading time: 3 minutes

Summarize the main points in the lecture, explaining how they cast doubt on those made in the reading

Part 1
獨立篇

Part 2
整合篇

With China emerging as the economic superpower in the international arena in the late 1990s, more and more students in the U.S. are eager to follow the trend of learning Mandarin Chinese. Many learners who dare to battle this notoriously difficult language hope that the ability to speak Mandarin will help them to acquire a promising job with more preponderance. The fad of learning Mandarin has reached an unprecedented climax, which is demonstrated not only by Mandarin classes offered in schools, but also by the support of Federal government policies. A government survey indicates that roughly 1,600 American public and private schools are teaching Mandarin.

While Chinese programs were mostly offered on the East and West Coasts ten years ago, Chinese lessons have surged in the heartland states in the Midwest and the South over the recent fewyears. The academic status of the language was formalized in 2007 when the College Board introduced the Mandarin Advanced Placement test, encouraging more high school students to learn Mandarin. The educational input is further publicized by the"1 Million Strong" initiative announced by the Obama administration in 2015, targeting the number of 1 million U.S. learners of Mandarin by 2020. Besides school and government efforts, the linguistic interest is also sparked by more Chinese movie stars appearing in Hollywood movies, such as Jackie Chan in "Shanghai Noon" and Jet Li in "the Mummy: Tomb of the Dragon Emperor".

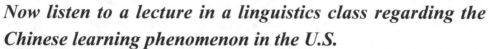

請聽與短文相關的課堂內容 ▶ *MP3 029*

Now listen to a lecture in a linguistics class regarding the Chinese learning phenomenon in the U.S.

（將聽到的重點，列在下列筆記欄內，並於練習後將記下的重點與高分範文的摘要重點作對照檢視是否記憶到關鍵重點。）

_____

_____

_____

_____

寫作實測

（在閱讀與播放音檔後，實際演練於 20 分鐘內完成整合題寫作，於電腦上打字完成 150-225 字數的英文。完成試題後請詳讀高分範文檢視與範文間的差異，強化應考實力）

_____

_____

_____

_____

整合能力強化① 訊息整合

比較「閱讀」和「聽力」講堂中內容的差異處，試著列出特點，比較特點後就能釐清主要差異或相似處，並著手開始寫作。

「閱讀」

* _____
* _____
* _____
* _____
* _____

「聽力」

* _____
* _____
* _____
* _____
* _____

整合訊息後，可以開始著手寫段落內容，寫完後可以與範文作對照。

* _____
* _____
* _____
* _____
* _____

① 這種觀念一部分是由商務菁英的故事建構而成，這些故事都是關於商務菁英搬移到富裕的中國城市。

_____

_____

ANS:

Such a notion was partially built up by the stories about the migration of business elites to affluent Chinese cities.

② 描繪中國為新興超級強權的報導不斷出現，且這些報導激勵了高中生和大學生學中文。

_____

_____

ANS:

The recurring reports illustrating China as the new superpower have motivated high school and college students to learn Chinese.

③ 相反地，學生對普通話的興趣不如大多數人想的那麼普及。

_____

_____

ANS:

On the contrary, students' interest in learning Mandarin is not as prevalent as some people think.

④ 就如同 1980 年代美國人學日文的熱潮已經消退，在美國教育體系裡，學普通話的風潮遲早也會消退。

_____

_____

ANS:

Just as the heat of learning Japanese in the 1980s had faded, it's only a matter of time that the trend of learning Mandarin will fade in the American educational system.

⑤ 首先，在過去十年內，由於州政府預算削減，許多公立學校不得不刪減外文課程。

_____

_____

ANS:

First, over the past decade, a lot of public schools had no choice but to eliminate foreign language classes owing to state budget cuts.

⑥ 既然學校被迫刪減曾經備受歡迎的歐語系課程，學生對外語課程的選擇自然地隨之被限縮。

_____

_____

ANS:

As schools are forced to cut down on their once popular European language classes, students simply have fewer foreign languages to choose from.

199

⑦ 對預算緊縮的學校而言，這些中國政府支援的老師和來自中國的補助的確緩解他們的預算窘況。

_____

_____

ANS:
Partially funding their salaries, which certainly came as a relieving subsidy to many schools with tight budgets.

⑧ 第二，這股語言熱潮似乎因歐巴馬總統在 2015 年宣布的「百萬強計畫」獲得加強。

_____

_____

ANS:
Secondly, the linguistic fever might be seemingly fortified by the"1 Million Strong" initiative announced by President Obama in 2015.

⑨ 我嚴重懷疑學生會因為看了這些明星演出，就被激勵出學中文的興趣，因為這些演員扮演的角色，仍是好萊塢對中國人的刻板印象，讓人聯想到李小龍扮演的那種刻板印象。

_____

_____

ANS:
I seriously doubt that students are motivated to learn Mandarin by watching their performances, since they still play the stereotype of Chinese reminiscent of Bruce Lee.

高分範文搶先看 ▶ *MP3 030*

Both the reading and the lecture describe the recent trend of acquiring Mandarin Chinese in the U.S. While the reading points out that the trend has achieved its zenith, the lecture opposes the main idea in the reading by arguing that U.S. students are not truly enthusiastic about learning Mandarin.

閱讀篇章及課堂演講都描述在美國近年來學習中文普通話的趨勢。雖然閱讀篇章指出此趨勢已達到近期的高峰，然而課堂演講反駁閱讀篇章的主題，且宣稱美國學生並非真的熱衷於中文學習。

To begin with, the professor elaborates on the reason why more and more students in public schools begin taking Mandarin classes, which he attributes to the budget cuts that prevented schools from offering as many foreign language classes as before. During the same period, many schools accepted Mandarin teachers who were funded partly by the Chinese government so that budget cut pressure might be eased. On the contrary, the reading merely states that Mandarin classes are increasing in many states.

首先，教授詳細闡述越來越多公立學校的學生開始上中文課的原因；他將其歸因於預算縮減，導致學校無法提供像以往那麼多的外文課程。同時間，許多學校接納了由中國政府部分資助的普通話老師，目的是舒緩預算刪減的壓力。相反地，閱讀篇章只單純描述普通話課程在許多州都持續增加。

Secondly, the professor rebuts the pervasiveness of the Mandarin learning phenomenon indicated by the "1 Million Strong" initiative mentioned in the reading. He explicates that even after the number of Mandarin learners in the U.S. reaches 1 million, it will be a relatively low percentage, hardly 2% in the entire student population.

第二，教授反駁了閱讀篇章中「百萬強計畫」暗示的學習普通話流行現象。他解釋即使美國的普通話學習者達到一百萬的數量，這仍是相對低的比率，幾乎勉強達到所
有學生人口的 2%。

Thirdly, the reading suggests that people are encouraged to learn Mandar in under the influence of Chinese movie stars in Hollywood, which the lecture refutes by claiming that those actors play stereotypical roles of Chinese characters.

第三，閱讀提及人們在好萊塢演出的中國電影明星影響下，會被激勵而開始學普通話。課堂演講針對此點駁斥，並主張那些演員擔任的仍是刻板印象的中國角色。

高分範文解析

關鍵句 ①

While the reading points out that the trend has reached its zenith, the lecture opposes the main idea in the reading by arguing that U.S. students are not truly enthusiastic about learning Mandarin.

解析

綜合題型在第一段須開門見山地描述閱讀和聽力內容兩者間的關聯。以上這句即是此篇範文的主旨句（thesis statement）。此兩篇題目的內容為主要觀點的牴觸，因此主旨句應使用表達兩個子句大意有所落差或對照的從屬連接詞，如 while、whereas、notwithstanding……等從屬連接詞。

關鍵句 ②

To begin with, the professor elaborates on the reason why more and more students in public schools begin taking Mandarin classes, which he attributes to the budget cuts that prevented schools from offering as many foreign language classes as before.

解析

作文要獲取高分必須盡量使用正式的動詞片語及複雜句。如以上範例使用動詞片語：elaborate on / attribute to / prevent ... from...，並利用形容詞子句濃縮課堂講述的重點。

閱讀短文中譯

請總結課堂講述的重點，並解釋它們如何對閱讀短文的重點提出質疑。

隨著中國以經濟強權之姿在九零年代後期的國際舞台上嶄露頭角，越來越多的美國學生渴望加入這股學習普通話中文的趨勢。許多敢挑戰這個以困難出名的語言的學習者希望的是，會說普通話的能力能幫助他們有更多優勢取得前景看好的工作。學習普通話的流行近來達到前所未有的高峰，從學校提供的普通話課程及聯邦政府政策的支持都彰顯了這趨勢。一項政府調查指出大約一千六百所美國公立及私立學校正在教普通話。十年前大部分的中文課程是在東岸及西岸地區被提供，然而在過去幾年，中文課程在中西部和南部各州急速增加。當大學入學委員會在 2007 年開始提供普通話入學檢定考，此舉奠定了普通話正式的學術地位，並鼓勵更多高中生學這語言。當歐巴馬政府在 2015 年宣佈了「百萬強計畫」，教育界的挹注更為眾所皆知，此計畫的目標是在 2020 年之前，提升美國境內的普通話學習者數量達到一百萬人。除了學校和政府的努力，更多中國電影明星參與好萊塢電影，如成龍演出「西域威龍（"Shanghai Noon"）」及李連杰演出「神鬼傳奇 3：龍帝之墓（"the Mummy: Tomb of the Dragon Emperor"）」，他們的表演也會激發對中文的興趣。

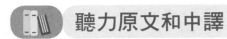

Now listen to a lecture in a linguistics class regarding the Chinese learning phenomenon in the U.S.

現在請聽一篇關於在美國中文學習現況的語言學課堂講述。

(Professor) Nowadays, a lot of Americans are under the impression that being able to speak Mandarin will help lead to abundant opportunities in the world's largest economy, China. Such a notion was partially built up by the stories about the migration of business elites to affluent Chinese cities. The recurring reports illustrating China as the new superpower have motivated high school and college students to learn Chinese. However, are the U.S. students actually zealous about learning Mandarin due to the reason aforementioned?

當今很多美國人都認為會說中文普通話能協助他們取得各式各樣在中國發展的機會，中國已是世界上最大的經濟體。這種觀念一部分是由商務菁英的故事建構而成，這些故事都是關於商務菁英搬移到富裕的中國城市。描繪中國為新興超級強權的報導不斷出現，且這些報導激勵了高中生和大學生學中文。然而，美國學生確實是因為以上提及的原因而熱衷於學習普通話嗎？

On the contrary, students' interest in learning Mandarin is not as prevalent as some people think, and just as the heat of learning Japanese in the 1980s had faded, it's only a matter of time that the trend of learning Mandarin will fade in the American educational system. First, over the past decade, a lot of public schools had no choice but to eliminate foreign language classes owing to state budget cuts. As schools are forced to cut down on their once popular European language classes, students simply have fewer foreign languages to choose from. Meanwhile, the Chinese government has been sending more Mandarin teachers to the U.S. and partially funding their salaries, which certainly came as a relieving subsidy to many schools with tight budgets.

相反地，學生對普通話的興趣不如大多數人想的那麼普及；就如同1980年代美國人學日文的熱潮已經消退，在美國教育體系裡，學普通話的風潮遲早也會消退。首先，在過去十年內，由於州政府預算削減，許多公立學校不得不刪減外文課程。既然學校被迫刪減曾經備受歡迎的歐語系課程，學生對外語課程的選擇自然地隨之被限縮。同時間中國政府派遣更多普通話老師到美國，並負責提供老師們的部份薪水。對預算緊縮的學校而言，這些中國政府支援的老師和來自中國的補助的確緩解他們的預算窘況。

Secondly, the linguistic fever might be seemingly fortified by the "1 Million Strong" initiative announced by President Obama in 2015. Let's not forget that the initiative is a collaboration between the Chinese and U.S. governments, with substantial resources from China. Moreover, 1 million seems a large number, yet it barely accounts for 2% of the number of all of the U.S. students. Lastly, Hollywood movies reinforce the illusion

206

of Chinese fever by incorporating Chinese actors, such as Jackie Chan and Jet Li, yet I seriously doubt that students are motivated to learn Mandarin by watching their performances, since they still play the stereotype of Chinese reminiscent of Bruce Lee. That is, they mainly serve to fight and kick.

第二，這股語言熱潮似乎因歐巴馬總統在 2015 年宣布的「百萬強計畫」獲得加強。別忘了這個計畫是中國及美國政府的合作計畫，由中方提供大量的資源。此外，一百萬似乎是一筆很大的數字，但只幾乎佔了美國總學生數量的 2%。最後，好萊塢電影融入中國電影明星，例如成龍和李連杰，加深了中文風潮的幻覺。我嚴重懷疑學生會因為看了這些明星演出，就被激勵出學中文的興趣，因為這些演員扮演的角色，仍是好萊塢對中國人的刻板印象，讓人聯想到李小龍扮演的那種刻板印象。也就是說，他們主要的功能是展現拳腳功夫。

UNIT 02

美國教育類：
網路教學的優點與缺點
The Advantages and Disadvantages of Online Learning

📖 INSTRUCTIONS

You have **20 minutes** to plan and write your response. Your response will be judged on the basis of the quality of your writing and on how well your response presents the points in the lecture and their relationships to the reading passage. Typically, an effective response will be 150 to 225 words.

Summarize the points made in the lecture you just heard, explaining how they cast doubt on points made in the reading.

Reading time: 3 minutes

Summarize the main points in the reading and lecture, explaining how they argue against each other

Since the advent of the Internet in the early 1980s, the Internet has exerted powerful hold of academia. Top universities, such as M.I.T, Harvard, and

208

Yale, have established numerous online courses for their students, while private online universities have mushroomed. The public can also take academic courses that were once confined in the scholarly circle by enrolling themselves in online programs collaborated by organizations, such as edX and Coursera, and renowned universities.

Nevertheless, newcomers in online classes might overlook the downside, or overestimate their own capability to acquire success in open courses. First, students underestimate the negative effect of little face-to-face interaction. They might find taking online classes is more like carrying out a monologue without immediate feedbacks from professors and classmates. Teachers cannot evaluate students' responses based on their facial expressions and body language, either. Secondly, even programs that utilize avatars to simulate face-to-face interactions, such as those on Second Life, might yield unexpected effects. For example, Ohio University once had to terminate its operation on Second Life when an avatar dressed as a gunman started random shooting.

Thirdly, contrary to popular impression, online courses require much more efforts than traditional ones. The amount of reading and reports usually surpasses that in conventional classes, and since students have to grapple with the reading and assignments by themselves most of the time, online courses require greater self-discipline and self-direction. For people who tend to procrastinate, they need to consider if they have adequate time-management skills to succeed. Moreover, in traditional courses, students have easier access to teachers' office hours and face-to-face meetings, which online courses have yet to achieve.

請聽與短文相關的課堂內容 ▶ *MP3 031*

Now listen to a lecture in an education class regarding online learning

（將聽到的重點，列在下列筆記欄內，並於練習後將記下的重點與高分範文的摘要重點作對照檢視是否記憶到關鍵重點。）

_____

_____

_____

_____

寫作實測

（在閱讀與播放音檔後，實際演練於 20 分鐘內完成整合題寫作，於電腦上打字完成 150-225 字數的英文。完成試題後請詳讀高分範文檢視與範文間的差異，強化應考實力）

_____

_____

_____

_____

整合能力強化① 訊息整合

比較「閱讀」和「聽力」講堂中內容的差異處，試著列出特點，比較特點後就能釐清主要差異或相似處，並著手開始寫作。

「閱讀」

* _____
* _____
* _____
* _____
* _____

「聽力」

* _____
* _____
* _____
* _____
* _____

整合訊息後，可以開始著手寫段落內容，寫完後可以與範文作對照。

* _____
* _____
* _____
* _____
* _____

① 不管你住在亞洲或非洲，只要你的資格達到入學標準，你就能舒適地在自己國家追求學士或碩士文憑。

_____

_____

ANS:

As long as your qualifications meet the admission criteria, you can pursue a bachelor or master degree at the comfort of staying in your home country.

② 此外，運用豐富的通訊軟體和虛擬教室，學生和老師間的互動不再被限制於平淡的討論版面，討論版面在網路發展的最早期就存在了。

_____

_____

ANS:

Further, with a wide variety of communication software and virtual classrooms, the interactions between students and teachers are no longer confined to plain discussion boards which can be traced to the earliest days of the Internet development.

③ 許多大學在虛擬教室方面已獲得成功，例如那些架設在第二人生網站的教室。

_____

Part 1
獨立篇

Part 2
整合篇

ANS:

Many universities have acquired success in virtual classrooms, such as those on Second Life.

④ 在第二人生的虛擬世界裡，使用者創造他們的替身，即代表他們身份的角色，並透過虛擬的豐富表情和手勢彼此互動。

ANS:

In the virtual world of Second Life, users create their avatars, representative figures of their identities, and interact with one another via abundant facial expressions and gestures simulated by their avatars.

⑤ 因為大學在第二人生網站建立建築物和城鎮，虛擬替身能造訪這些地方並認識彼此，促進社群的感覺。

ANS:

Universities are able to foster a sense of community on Second Life because they build buildings and towns where avatars visit and acquaint themselves with others.

⑥ 一項統計研究顯示網路課程學生的統計數據和傳統課堂內的學生

非常不同。

_____

_____

ANS:

A statistical research has indicated that the demographics of online students is very different from that in traditional classrooms.

⑦ 網路課程的學生大部份是有小孩的已婚者或離婚者，或是為了提升職涯來兼職上課的專業人士。

_____

_____

ANS:

Most of them are married or divorced with children, or professionals who take part-time classes to advance their careers.

⑧ 對這些人而言，在傳統大學可能不容易交到朋友，但是當他們上網路課程，他們更有可能遇到興趣，職業及經歷類似的人。

_____

_____

ANS:

For these individuals, it might be hard for them to make friends in traditional universities, yet while they take classes online, they have more access to meeting people with similar interests, careers, and experiences.

⑨ 他們也能滿足對學業的追求，同時照顧家庭，並藉由在虛擬教室和來自世界各地的學生互動，增長國際觀。

Part 1
獨立篇

Part 2
整合篇

_____

_____

ANS:

Also, they can fulfill their academic pursuit while attending to their families as well as gaining internationalized vision by interacting with students from around the world in virtual classrooms.

The reading and listening passages present contrasting views of online education, with the former focusing on disadvantages and the latter focusing on advantages.

閱讀篇章及課堂講述呈現對網路課程的相反看法，前者著重缺點而後者著重優點。

The first disadvantage of online classes is the lack of in person interaction. Students tend to feel that their contribution to online classes is carried out in a one way direction. The second drawback concerns the undesired effect of applying avatars in virtual classrooms. Avatars with ill intentions might cause a disturbance in on-line classrooms. The third drawback is that more self-discipline and self-guidance are necessary when people take online courses.

網路課程的第一個缺點是缺乏親身互動。學生通常覺得他們對網路課程的付出是單向的。第二個缺點是關於在虛擬教室運用替身所帶來的意料之外的效應。不懷好意的替身可能對網路教室造成困擾。第三個缺點是當人們上網路課程時，需要更多自我紀律和自我導引。

The lecture refutes the reading by raising three advantages. It first points out that on-line courses allow students not residing in the U.S. to pursue degrees without traveling away from home. Next, the lecture draws on the example of virtual classrooms on Second Life to explain that vibrant

216

interaction and a sense of community can be enhanced.

課堂講述提出三個優點駁斥閱讀篇章。它首先指出網路課程讓不住在美國的學生不須離家遠遊就能追求學位。其次，課堂講述引用位於第二人生網站的虛擬教室為例，解釋活潑的互動和社群的感覺能被加強。

Lastly, by raising the demographics of students, the lecture indicates that elder students are more capable of striking a balance between family and work and acquainting similar-minded friends in the online setting.

最後，課堂講述提出學生的人口統計數據，指出在網路情境裡，年紀較長的學生比較能取得家庭和工作的平衡，並結交興趣類似的朋友。

高分範文解析

關鍵句 ①

Students tend to feel that their contribution to online classes is carried out in a one-way direction.

解析

此句的主要動詞是動詞片語 tend to V.，傾向，類似詞有 have the tendency to V.，be inclined to V.，be prone to V.。受詞是 that 導引出的名詞子句。名詞子句直到句尾，子句的動詞因為搭配主詞 their contribution，所以使用被動語態 is carried out。

關鍵句 ②

Lastly, by raising the demographics of students, the lecture indicates that elder students are more capable of striking a balance between family and work and acquainting similar-minded friends in the online setting.

解析

主要動詞 indicates 的受詞是 that 導引出的名詞子句。名詞子句中，介系詞 of 之後有兩個由對等連接詞 and 連接的動名詞當受詞：striking ... 及 acquainting。

閱讀短文中譯

請總結閱讀短文和課堂講述的重點，並解釋它們如何互相駁斥。

自從在 1980 年代初期問世，網路對學術圈已產生強大的影響。頂尖大學，例如麻省理工學院、哈佛大學和耶魯大學，都為了學生設立許多網路課程，同時間私立的網路大學則迅速增加。大眾也能報名知名大學和 edX 及 Coursera 等組織合作的課程，參與以往僅限於學術圈的學術課程。

然而，網路課程的新使用者可能忽略了其負面，或高估了他們自己能在網路課程成功的能力。首先，學生低估了幾乎沒有面對面互動的負面效應。他們可能會發現上網路課程比較像是進行一場缺乏教授和同學的立即回應的獨白。老師也無法以學生的表情和肢體語言評量他們的反應。第二，即使是利用虛擬替身模擬親身互動的課程，例如在第二人生網站上的課程，可能產生意料之外的效應。例如，當一個裝扮為槍手的替身開始開槍掃射時，俄亥俄大學曾經必須中止他們在第二人生網站上的運作。

第三，與大眾印象不同的是，網路課程比傳統課程需要更多的努力。閱讀和報告的數量通常比傳統課堂多，而且既然大部份的時間學生必須單獨進行閱讀和作業，網路課程需要更多的自我紀律和自我導引。對容易拖延的人而言，他們需要考慮是否有足夠的時間管理技巧能達到成功。此外，在傳統課程，學生更容易取得老師的辦公會面時間和面對面開會的機會，而這些是網路課程仍無法比擬的。

Now listen to a lecture in an education class regarding online learning

現在請聽一篇關於網路教學的教育學課堂講述。

(Professor) There are numerous advantages to online learning. Today the lecture will focus on the benefits of online courses offered by higher education institutes in the U.S.

網路課程有許多優點。今天的課堂講述著重於美國高等教育機構提供的網路課程所帶來的益處。

The first that comes to mind is probably the worldwide access. No matter you live in Asia or Africa, as long as your qualifications meet the admission criteria, you can pursue a bachelor or master degree at the comfort of staying in your home country.

第一個讓人想到的優點很可能是全球普及化。不管你住在亞洲或非洲，只要你的資格達到入學標準，你就能舒適地在自己國家追求學士或碩士文憑。

Part 1
獨立篇

Part 2
整合篇

Further, with a wide variety of communication software and virtual classrooms, the interactions between students and teachers are no longer confined to plain discussion boards which can be traced to the earliest days of the Internet development.

此外，運用豐富的通訊軟體和虛擬教室，學生和老師間的互動不再被限制於平淡的討論版面，討論版面在網路發展的最早期就存在了。

Many universities have acquired success in virtual classrooms, such as those on Second Life. In the virtual world of Second Life, users create their avatars, representative figures of their identities, and interact with one another via abundant facial expressions and gestures simulated by their avatars.

許多大學在虛擬教室方面已獲得成功，例如那些架設在第二人生網站的教室。在第二人生的虛擬世界裡，使用者創造他們的替身，即代表他們身份的角色，並透過虛擬的豐富表情和手勢彼此互動。

Universities are able to foster a sense of community on Second Life because they build buildings and towns where avatars visit and acquaint themselves with others.

因為大學在第二人生網站建立建築物和城鎮，虛擬替身能造訪這些地方並認識彼此，促進社群的感覺。

Moreover, long-distance learning is particularly appropriate for adults who have to take care of their family and work at the same time.

另外，遠距教學特別適合必須照顧家庭及同時間工作的成年人。

A statistical research has indicated that the demographics of online students is very different from that in traditional classrooms.

一項統計研究顯示網路課程學生的統計數據和傳統課堂內的學生非常不同。

Most of them are married or divorced with children, or professionals who take part-time classes to advance their careers. For these individuals, it might be hard for them to make friends in traditional universities, yet while they take classes online, they have more access to meeting people with similar interests, careers, and experiences.

網路課程的學生大部份是有小孩的已婚者或離婚者，或是為了提升職涯來兼職上課的專業人士。對這些人而言，在傳統大學可能不容易交到朋友，但是當他們上網路課程，他們更有可能遇到興趣，職業及經歷類似的人。

Also, they can fulfill their academic pursuit while attending to their families as well as gaining internationalized vision by interacting with students from around the world in virtual classrooms.

他們也能滿足對學業的追求，同時照顧家庭，並藉由在虛擬教室和來自世界各地的學生互動，增長國際觀。

UNIT 03

美國教育類：
1960 年代的嬉皮運動
The Hippie Movement in the 1960s

INSTRUCTIONS

You have **20 minutes** to plan and write your response. Your response will be judged on the basis of the quality of your writing and on how well your response presents the points in the lecture and their relationships to the reading passage. Typically, an effective response will be 150 to 225 words.

Summarize the points made in the lecture you just heard, explaining how they cast doubt on points made in the reading.

Reading time: 3 minutes

Briefly paraphrase the origin of hippies, and summarize the contradictory arguments in the reading and the lecture.

The 1960s was a period when the counterculture burgeoned in America.

The most well-known lifestyle of the counterculture was hippies. Even now the hippie lifestyle is sometimes portrayed in Hollywood movies, in which hippies are presented with the image of having long hair, casual attitude, and taking drugs. Yet, if we truly understand the origin of hippies, we will understand that there were a deeper root of this lifestyle and some philosophy behind it.

The predecessors of hippies were the generation a decade earlier known as the Beats. The fundamental philosophy of the Beats includes disbelief in traditional American values, attempts to create new social standards, and rejection of materialism. At first, the Beats wanted to remain inconspicuous and keep themselves underground. However, as more and more followers of the Beats began to speak out about political issues, by 1960, the lifestyle of the Beats had transformed into the one we now call hippies.

Though hippies were sometimes criticized for their use of drugs, they indeed made significant contributions to the American society. First, in response to the U.S. involvement in the Vietnam War, the hippie lifestyle elevated itself into the movement against war. Hippies often preached love, not war, and identified themselves with the peace sign. Also, they supported the Civil Rights Movement led by Dr. Martin Luther King, and held many demonstrations against war and racial injustice, promoting equal rights for minorities. They also questioned the government's treatment of Native Americans. Last but not least, their most long-lasting legacy was raising the awareness of how humans impacted nature. Hippies' emphasis on green energy helped foster the green awareness.

Now listen to a lecture in an American history class on the same topic you just read about

（將聽到的重點，列在下列筆記欄內，並於練習後將記下的重點與高分範文的摘要重點作對照檢視是否記憶到關鍵重點。）

_____

_____

_____

_____

_____

寫作實測

（在閱讀與播放音檔後，實際演練於 20 分鐘內完成整合題寫作，於電腦上打字完成 150-225 字數的英文。完成試題後請詳讀高分範文檢視與範文間的差異，強化應考實力）

_____

_____

_____

_____

整合能力強化① 訊息整合

比較「閱讀」和「聽力」講堂中內容的差異處，試著列出特點，比較特點後就能釐清主要差異或相似處，並著手開始寫作。

「閱讀」

- _____
- _____
- _____
- _____
- _____

「聽力」

- _____
- _____
- _____
- _____
- _____

整合訊息後，可以開始著手寫段落內容，寫完後可以與範文作對照。

- _____
- _____
- _____
- _____
- _____

① 當美國人聊到 1960 年代和 1970 年代初期，兩個事件一定會被提出，一個是越戰，另一個是嬉皮運動。

_____

_____

ANS:

When Americans talk about the 1960s and early 1970s, two events will almost certainly be raised; one is the Vietnam War and the other is the hippie movement.

② 嬉皮運動常被視為那時年輕人對傳統美國價值的象徵性反抗，且嬉皮的強烈反戰意識及對越戰的抗議活動受到廣泛的媒體報導。

_____

_____

ANS:

The hippie movement, often seen as a symbolic rebellion of the youth at that time against the conventional values of the U.S. society, received wide media coverage due to hippies' strong anti-war sentiment and their demonstrations against the Vietnam War.

③ 性解放及大麻和其他毒品的使用增加也是引起大眾注意的原因。

_____

_____

ANS:

Other reasons for public attention were sexual liberation and the increasing use of marijuana and other drugs.

④ 明顯地，嬉皮跟重視個人主義，探索性意識和堅持和平主義這些特色連結在一起。

_____

_____

ANS:

Evidently, hippies were associated with an emphasis on individualism, experimentation of sexuality, and insistence of pacifism.

⑤ 有些嬉皮最初的確遵守他們的理念，但如同我的論點會顯示的，嬉皮生活的現實面不像他們最初預想的那麼理想。

_____

_____

ANS:

Some hippies did stick to their philosophy initially, yet as my argument will indicate, the reality of the hippie lifestyle was not as ideal as they had envisioned.

⑥ 事實上，有研究顯示在 1960 年代，不到百分之十的美國青年是嬉皮。

_____

_____

ANS:

In fact, research has suggested that no more than 10 percent of American youths in the 1960s were hippies.

⑦ 大部分美國年輕人維持了傳統的生活風格，也延續了他們父母的中產階級文化。

_____

_____

ANS:

Conventional lifestyles were maintained by most young Americans, who continued their parents' middle-class culture.

⑧ 其次，嬉皮對個人主義的堅持矛盾地導致他們傾向於集體生活的形式，因為寂寞和孤立跟主流社會是疏離的。

_____

_____

ANS:

Next, hippies' insistence on individualism paradoxically caused their preference to live in groups owing to loneliness and isolation from the mainstream society.

⑨ 雖然他們的理念核心是忠於自我，他們偏好住在被稱為公社的社區，而迷幻藥和隨意性愛在公社更容易取得。

_____

_____

ANS:

Although the core of their philosophy is being true to oneself, they prefer living in communities known as communes where psychedelic drugs and casual sex became more available.

Before hippies surfaced as a dominant part of the American counterculture in the 1960s, they were pioneered by another generation called the Beats in the 1950s. The ideas of the Beats remained with hippies except that hippies were more enthusiastic about politics.

在嬉皮於 1960 年代的美國反主流文化嶄露頭角之前，他們的先驅是 1950 年代的節奏世代。嬉皮維持節奏世代的理念，只是嬉皮對政治比較熱衷。

According to the reading, the culture of the hippies left a positive legacy despite occasional criticism of their drug usage. First, as the U.S. government became more involved in the Vietnam War, the lifestyle of the hippies became more related to an antiwar movement. Secondly, the hippies allied themselves with the Civil Rights Movement and advocated racial equality. Most crucially, hippies emphasized being friendly with the Earth, and their attitude was influential in raising subsequent awareness of environmental protection.

根據閱讀篇章，嬉皮文化留下正面的文化遺產，盡管偶爾有對他們使用毒品的批評。首先，當美國政府在越戰牽涉越深，嬉皮的生活方式跟反戰運動的關係就越密切。第二，嬉皮支持民權運動並倡導種族平等。最重要的是，嬉皮強調對地球友善，他們的態度對之後提升環保意識有所影響。

Contrary to the main argument of the reading, the lecture casts doubt on the hippies' legacy. The professor first explains that the media at that time enlarged the influence of the hippie movement; the truth was that most American youths still followed a traditional lifestyle. Furthermore, she points out that hippies acted against their own philosophy of individualism, since they preferred living in communes where casual sex and drug usage became more prevalent.

課堂講述與閱讀篇章的主要論點相反，對嬉皮的文化遺產提出質疑。教授首先解釋當時的媒體將嬉皮運動的影響力放大了。事實上大部分的美國青年仍然遵循傳統生活方式。此外，她指出嬉皮的行為牴觸他們對個人主義的理念，因為他們偏好住在團體公社裡，且在公社隨意性愛和使用毒品的現象更普遍。

Lastly, she criticized the double standard of the hippies' attitude toward sex in that female hippies often suffered more than men when faced with unwanted pregnancy due to the lack of birth control pills.

最後，她批評嬉皮對性愛態度的雙重標準，因為缺乏避孕藥，當被迫面對意外懷孕時，女性嬉皮受的折磨比男性多。

Part 1
獨立篇

Part 2
整合篇

233

關鍵句 ①

Before hippies surfaced as a dominant part of the American counterculture in the 1960s, they were pioneered by another generation called the Beats in the 1950s. The ideas of the Beats remained with hippies except that hippies were more enthusiastic about politics.

解析

當題目有要求簡短重述閱讀篇章或課堂講述的某些知識時，此部分應構成第 一段的內容，且所佔的篇幅不超過整篇文章的三分之一。

關鍵句 ②

According to the reading, the culture of the hippies left a positive legacy despite occasional criticism of their drug usage. ...Contrary to the main argument of the reading, the lecture casts doubt on the hippies' legacy.

解析

此單元題目屬於 contrast 類型：課堂講述駁斥閱讀篇章的主要論點。每段的主題句（topic sentences）應該要將閱讀和聽力兩個篇章主要觀點的差異闡述清楚，如使用以下片語：contrary to N、in contrast to N、torefute N、to rebut N。當重點之間呼應的關係不明顯時（例如閱讀稱讚嬉皮對環保的影響，但課堂講述並未提及環保），可採取一段總結閱讀篇章，另一段總結課堂講述的結構。

閱讀短文中譯

請將嬉皮的起源簡短的換句話說，並總結閱讀短文和課堂講述互相駁斥的論點。

在美國 1960 年代是反主流文化急速發展的時代。反主流文化中最知名的生活方式是嬉皮。即使是現在嬉皮風格偶爾也被好萊塢電影呈現，將嬉皮呈現為留著長髮，態度隨意和吸毒的形象。但是，如果我們真的懂嬉皮的起源，我們會知道這種生活方式有較深的根基及背後有一些哲理。

嬉皮的先驅是十年前的世代，他們被稱為節奏世代。節奏世代的基本哲理包含對傳統美國價值的不信任，嘗試創造新的社會標準，及反對物質主義。最初，節奏世代想保持低調，維持地下活動的形式。然而，當越來越多節奏世代發表對政治議題的看法，到了 1960 年代，節奏世代的生活方式轉化成我們現稱的嬉皮。

雖然嬉皮有時因為使用毒品而被批評，他們的確對美國社會做出重要貢獻。首先，針對美國對越戰的干涉，嬉皮風格被提升至反戰運動。嬉皮常常宣導愛的精神，反對戰爭，並以和平圖示表達身份。另外，他們支持馬丁·路德·金恩博士領導的民權運動，舉辦許多反戰及反對種族不平等的示威活動，促進少數族群的平權。他們也質疑政府對待美洲原住民的方式。最後，他們對後代影響最深的貢獻是提高人類如何影響大自然的意識。嬉皮對節約能源的重視協助培養了環保意識。

Now listen to a lecture in an American history class on the same topic you just read about

現在請聽一篇與閱讀篇章一樣主題的美國歷史課堂講述。

(Professor) When Americans talk about the 1960s and early 1970s, two events will almost certainly be raised; one is the Vietnam War and the other is the hippie movement.

當美國人聊到 1960 年代和 1970 年代初期，兩個事件一定會被提出，一個是越戰，另一個是嬉皮運動。

The hippie movement, often seen as a symbolic rebellion of the youth at that time against the conventional values of the U.S. society, received wide media coverage due to hippies' strong anti-war sentiment and their demonstrations against the Vietnam War.

嬉皮運動常被視為那時年輕人對傳統美國價值的象徵性反抗，且嬉皮的強烈反戰意識及對越戰的抗議活動受到媒體的廣泛報導。

Other reasons for public attention were sexual liberation and the increasing use of marijuana and other drugs. Evidently, hippies were associated with an emphasis on individualism, experimentation of sexuality, and insistence on pacifism.

性解放及大麻和其他毒品的使用增加也是引起大眾注意的原因。明顯地，嬉皮跟重視個人主義，探索性意識和堅持和平主義這些特色連結在一起。

Some hippies did stick to their philosophy initially, yet as my argument will indicate, the reality of the hippie lifestyle was not as ideal as they had envisioned. Also, I think it is an overstatement to say that all hippies left a positive legacy.

有些嬉皮最初的確遵守他們的理念，但如同我的論點會顯示的，嬉皮生活的現實面不像他們最初預想的那麼理想。而且，我認為說所有嬉皮都留下正面影響，這是誇張的說法。

First, the influence of hippies was magnified by the media. In fact, research has suggested that no more than 10 percent of American youths in the 1960s were hippies.

首先，嬉皮的影響力被媒體誇大了。事實上，有研究顯示在 1960 年代，不到百分之十的美國青年是嬉皮。

Conventional lifestyles were maintained by most young Americans, who continued their parents' middle-class culture. Next, hippies' insistence on individualism paradoxically caused their preference to live in groups owing to loneliness and isolation from the mainstream society.

大部分美國年輕人維持了傳統的生活風格，也延續了他們父母的中產階級文化。其次，嬉皮對個人主義的堅持矛盾地導致他們傾向集體生活的形式，因為寂寞和孤立跟主流社會是疏離的。

Although the core of their philosophy is being true to oneself, they prefer living in communities known as communes where psychedelic drugs and casual sex became more available.

雖然他們的理念核心是忠於自我，他們偏好住在被稱為公社的社區，而迷幻藥和隨意性愛在公社更容易取得。

Finally, the idea of casual sex or free love held double standards for men and women because of the lack of birth control.

最後，因為缺乏避孕的關係，隨意性愛的觀念對男性和女性有雙重標準。

Birth control pills were first sold in 1960, so they were not readily available for single women, which means that as undesired pregnancy happened, hippie women were usually the ones feeling plagued, not hippie men.

避孕藥品在 1960 年才開始販售，所以那時單身女性無法輕易取得這種藥品，意味著當意外懷孕時，嬉皮族群的女性通常是備受折磨的，而不是男性。

美國歷史類：
美國內戰之後的重建時期
The Reconstruction Period after the Civil War

📖 INSTRUCTIONS

You have *20 minutes* to plan and write your response. Your response will be judged on the basis of the quality of your writing and on how well your response presents the points in the lecture and their relationships to the reading passage. Typically, an effective response will be 150 to 225 words.

Summarize the points made in the lecture you just heard, explaining how they cast doubt on points made in the reading.

Reading time: 3 minutes

The Reconstruction period began in 1865, right after the end of the Civil War. It spanned over 12 years, ending in 1877. With the end of the Civil War, President Lincoln started to draft schemes to reunite a nation that had been separated by racism and torn apart by war. Successes had arisen from

Reconstruction and they can be categorized into three aspects: political, social, and economic.

In the political aspect, the most important success was that the concept of the United States as one unified nation was finally consolidated. Reconstruction brought the Southern states back to the Union. Although many white Southerners were against the idea of reconstructuring the South, political reforms were administered, notably the new constitutional amendments. The 13th Amendment to the Constitution officially ended slavery, and 15th Amendment offered the equal right to vote to all citizens.

In the social aspect, education programs for freed slaves were initiated by the Federal government and charitable organizations, and thus literacy was greatly improved among freed slaves. Freed slaves also gained more autonomy in their cultural institutions and churches. Under the protection of the Constitution, they were able to reunite with their families and keep their personal property.

Lastly, the economy in the South revitalized as the Federal government built new railroads and hospitals, and new industries, such as steel and lumber, began to prosper. A small scale of land reform was carried out, allowing freed slaves to farm on their own land.

請聽與短文相關的課堂內容 ▶ *MP3 035*

Now listen to a lecture in an American history class regarding the Reconstruction Period

（將聽到的重點，列在下列筆記欄內，並於練習後將記下的重點與高分範文的摘要重點作對照檢視是否記憶到關鍵重點。）

_____

_____

_____

_____

_____

寫作實測

（在閱讀與播放音檔後，實際演練於 20 分鐘內完成整合題寫作，於電腦上打字完成 150-225 字數的英文。完成試題後請詳讀高分範文檢視與範文間的差異，強化應考實力）

_____

_____

_____

_____

_____

整合能力強化① 訊息整合

比較「閱讀」和「聽力」講堂中內容的差異處，試著列出特
點，比較特點後就能釐清主要差異或相似處，並著手開始寫
作。

「閱讀」

- _____
- _____
- _____
- _____
- _____

「聽力」

- _____
- _____
- _____
- _____
- _____

整合訊息後，可以開始著手寫段落內容，寫完後可以與範文作對照。

- _____
- _____
- _____
- _____
- _____

① 多年來,歷史學家一直爭辯重建時期是導致成功還是失敗。我認為失敗無疑地多於成功。

_____

_____

ANS:
Over the years, historians have debated whether the Reconstruction generated successes or failures. In my opinion, the failures undoubtedly outweigh the successes.

② 政治上,美國似乎是統一國家了,且奴隸終於被解放。然而,這只是聯邦政府以立法改革建構出的假象。

_____

_____

ANS:
Politically, the U.S. seemed to be one unified nation, and slaves were finally emancipated. However, that was just a façade constructed by the Federal government with legislative reforms.

③ 在南方各州,大部分白人,尤其是富人和菁英人士,致力於翻轉那些改革。的確,在憲法層次,奴隸制度結束了。

_____

_____

ANS:

Deep down in the Southern states, most white people, especially the wealthy and the elites, strove to undo the reforms. It is true that slavery ended on the constitutional level.

④ 但南方各州通過限制非裔美國人大部份權利的法律，稱為黑人規範，這些法律對他們的限制包含跨種族婚姻，擔任陪審團成員的權力，投票權和言論自由。

_____

_____

ANS:

Yet the legislature in every southern state passed laws, the Black Codes, to restrict most rights of African Americans, including interracial marriage, the right to serve on a jury, voting rights, and freedom of speech.

⑤ 因此，非裔美國人直到 1960 年代的民權運動才能獲得真正的平權。有些人可能主張在重建時期，奴隸解放的情況被改善了。

_____

_____

ANS:

As a result, African Americans could not attain true equal rights until much later during the Civil Rights Movement in the 1960s. Some might argue that slave emancipation was improved during the Reconstruction.

⑥ 事實上，改善只發生在相當少的被解放奴隸身上，不管是教育或經濟方面。大部分在南方被解放的奴隸仍未受教育且陷於貧窮。

_____

_____

ANS:
The truth is that such improvement happened to a relatively low proportion of emancipated slaves, no matter educationally or financially. Most freed slaves in the South remained uneducated and trapped in poverty.

⑦ 他們的生活因為暴力威脅每下愈況，威脅來自三 K 黨這個種族歧視的團體，三 K 指的是 Klu Klux Klan。在社會上，被解放的奴隸必須面對充斥更多敵意的環境，因為三 K 黨採取極端暴力的手段攻擊和謀殺被解放的奴隸及其支持者。

_____

_____

ANS:
Their living condition was worsened by the violent threats from a racist group called the KKK, which stands for the Klu Klux Klan. Socially, freed slaves had to face a more hostile environment since the Klan resorted to extreme violence to attack and murder freed slaves and their allies.

⑧ 至於經濟上，白人和黑人都經歷痛苦。農業是南方經濟的支柱，但是奴隸被解放後，農場上的員工減少了。

_____

ANS:

In terms of economy, both whites and blacks suffered. Agriculture was the backbone of southern economy, yet after the Emancipation, the workers on plantations reduced.

The lecture presents three arguments regarding the political, social and economic areas of the Reconstruction period to refute the arguments in the reading. Whereas the reading argues for the successes of Reconstruction, the lecture contends otherwise.

課堂講述呈現關於重建時期的政治，社會和經濟方面的三個論點，以反駁閱讀篇章的論點。閱讀篇章主張重建時期是成功的，然而課堂講述的主張是相反的。

First, in terms of political reforms, the reading emphasizes that Amendemts to the Constitution legalized equal voting rights for all citizens and put an end to slavery. On the contrary, the lecture points out that new laws passed in the southern states, called the Black Codes, undermined the effects of the constitutional reform for freed slaves' rights were dramatically restrained.

首先，在政治改革上，閱讀篇章強調憲法修正案將所有公民的平等投票權法制化，並終結奴隸制度。相反地，課堂講述指出在南方各州通過的黑人規範新法律削弱了憲法改革的效應，因此被解放的奴隸的權力被大幅限制了。

Secondly, regarding the social aspect, the lecture contends that freed slaves faced more hostility due to the violent intimidation from the KKK, a racist group.

Although the reading mentions that education was provided for freed slaves, the lecture explains that most former slaves did not benefit from it.

第二，關於社會方面，課堂講述主張被解放的奴隸因為種族歧視團體三 K 黨的暴力威脅，而面對更多敵意。雖然閱讀篇章提到被解放的奴隸曾被提供教育，課堂講述解釋大部分的被解放奴隸並未因此獲益。

Thirdly, the lecture describes that both whites and blacks went through difficult times of economic recession; in contrast, the reading merely mentions an improvement for freed slaves, a limited scale of land reform.

According to the lecture, white plantation owners faced the decrease of workers, and new industries did not enhance prosperity, since they did not occupy most of the southern economy. Many emancipated slaves still returned to work for their previous owners and lived in destitution.

第三，課堂講述描述白人和黑人都經歷經濟蕭條的苦日子。反之，閱讀篇章只提及對被解放奴隸的改善，即小規模的土地改革。根據課堂講述，農場的白人地主面對員工減少，而且新產業並未促進繁榮，因為它們不是占了南方經濟的大部分。許多被解放的奴隸仍然回去替前主人工作且活在赤貧中。

關鍵句 ①

Whereas the reading argues for the successes of Reconstruction, the lecture contends otherwise.

解析

第一段的兩句都屬於此篇範文的主旨句（thesis statement）。此單元的閱讀篇章和課堂講述各提出三個相反的論點，而關鍵句 1 更精簡地闡明兩者互相駁斥的關係，otherwise（*adv.*）意近 contrarily。

關鍵句 ②

On the contrary, the lecture points out that new laws passed in the southern states, called the Black Codes, undermined the effects of the constitutional reform for freed slaves' rights were dramatically restrained.

解析

轉折副詞 on the contrary 導引出與上一句意思相反的下文，that ...直到句尾是名詞子句，當作 points out 的受詞。名詞子句中的 passed 是過去分詞，修飾 n ew l aws，表被動語態。名詞子句的主要動詞是 undermined，削弱，而 for 是表原因的連接詞，在學術文章常代替 because。

閱讀短文中譯

請總結課堂講述的重點，並解釋它們如何對閱讀短文的重點提出質疑。

重建時期在 1865 年美國內戰結束後旋即開始。它持續了十二年，於 1877 年結束。隨著內戰結束，林肯總統開始起草如何團結被種族主義和戰爭所分裂的國家方案。重建時期獲得成功，而那些成功可被分類為三方面：政治，社會和經濟。

在政治方面，最重要的成功是美國是統一的國家這個觀念，終於受到鞏固。重建時期將南方各州和北方聯盟整合。雖然很多南方白人反對重建南方這個概念，政治改革仍被執行，值得注意的是新的憲法修正案。第十三號修正案正式終結奴隸制度，而第十五號修正案提供所有公民平等的投票權。

在社會方面，聯邦政府和慈善機構開始提供教育課程給被解放的黑奴，因此他們的識字能力大幅提升。被解放的黑奴也在他們的文化機構和教堂獲得較多的自治權。在憲法的保護之下，他們得以和家人團圓並持有私人財產。

最後，隨著聯邦政府在當地興建新鐵路和醫院，南方的經濟復甦了，而且新產業，例如鋼鐵和木材業，開始發達。小規模的土地改革讓被解放的奴隸能在私有地上耕種。

Now listen to a lecture in an American history class regarding the Reconstruction Period

現在請聽一篇關於重建時期的美國歷史課堂講述。

(Professor) Over the years, historians have debated whether the Reconstruction generated successes or failures. In my opinion, the failures undoubtedly outweigh the successes.

多年來，歷史學家一直爭辯重建時期是導致成功，還是失敗。我認為失敗無疑地多於成功。

Politically, the U.S. seemed to be one unified nation, and slaves were finally emancipated. However, that was just a façade constructed by the Federal government with legislative reforms.

政治上，美國似乎是統一國家了，且奴隸終於被解放。然而，這只是聯邦政府以立法改革建構出的假象。

Deep down in the Southern states, most white people, especially the wealthy and the elites, strove to undo the reforms. It is true that slavery ended on the constitutional level, yet the legislature in every southern state passed laws, the Black Codes, to restrict most rights of African Americans, including interracial marriage, the right to serve on a jury, voting rights, and freedom of speech.

在南方各州，大部分白人，尤其是富人和菁英人士，致力於翻轉那些改革。的確，在憲法層次，奴隸制度結束了，但南方各州通過限制非裔美國人大部份權利的法律，稱為黑人規範，這些法律對他們的限制包含跨種族婚姻，擔任陪審團成員的權力，投票權和言論自由。

As a result, African Americans could not attain true equal rights until much later during the Civil Rights Movement in the 1960s.

因此，非裔美國人直到 1960 年代的民權運動才能獲得真正的平權。

Some might argue that slave emancipation was improved during the Reconstruction. The truth is that such improvement happened to a relatively low proportion of emancipated slaves, no matter educationally or financially.

有些人可能主張在重建時期，奴隸解放的情況被改善了。事實上，改善只發生在相當少的被解放奴隸身上，不管是教育或經濟方面。

Most freed slaves in the South remained uneducated and trapped in poverty. Their living condition was worsened by the violent threats from a racist group called the KKK, which stands for the Klu Klux Klan.

大部分在南方被解放的奴隸仍未受教育且陷於貧窮。他們的生活因為暴力威脅每下愈況，威脅來自三 K 黨這個種族歧視的團體，三 K 指的是 Klu Klux Klan。

Socially, freed slaves had to face a more hostile environment since the Klan resorted to extreme violence to attack and murder freed slaves and their allies.

在社會上，被解放的奴隸必須面對充斥更多敵意的環境，因為三 K 黨採取極端暴力的手段攻擊和謀殺被解放的奴隸及其支持者。

In terms of economy, both whites and blacks suffered. Agriculture was the backbone of southern economy, yet after the Emancipation, the workers on plantations reduced. New industries, like steel, did not boost the economy since they composed a minor percentage, compared with agriculture.

至於經濟上，白人和黑人都經歷痛苦。農業是南方經濟的支柱，但是奴隸被解放後，農場上的員工減少了。新產業，像是鋼鐵業，無法刺激經濟，因為跟農業相比的話，新產業只占少部分。

Land reform was not widespread, either, and lots of former slaves went back to work on plantations for their former masters under a new system, sharecropping, which tied workers to the yields of their crops on rented land. Therefore, freed slaves remained in debt and poverty.

土地改革並未普及，許多被解放的奴隸回去農場替他們的前主人工作，他們在佃農這個新制度下工作，佃農制度使他們必須在租來的土地上，依賴農作收成數量獲得收入。因此，被解放的奴隸仍陷於債務和貧窮。

UNIT
05

美國文學類：
區域主義文學及馬克‧吐溫的《哈克歷險記》

Regionalism and Mark Twain's The Adventures of Huckleberry Finn

 INSTRUCTIONS

You have *20 minutes* to plan and write your response. Your response will be judged on the basis of the quality of your writing and on how well your response presents the points in the lecture and their relationships to the reading passage. Typically, an effective response will be 150 to 225 words.

Summarize the points made in the lecture you just heard, explaining how they cast doubt on points made in the reading.

Reading time: 3 minutes

Summarize the main features of The Adventures of Huckleberry Finn described in the lecture, and explain why it belongs to the style of regionalism described in the reading

Regionalism is a style of literature popular in the late 19th century American society. Famous novels that employ regionalism include Mark Twain's *The Adventures of Huckleberry Finn* and Kate Chopin's *Awakening*, and *The House of Mirth* by Edith Wharton. It also arose from the opposition to Romanticism, a previously dominant style, and sought to respond to radical social and political changes in America in the 19th century, including the end of the Civil War, the abolition of slavery, and the Industrial Revolution.

Unlike Romanticism that had emphasized stormy emotion and extravagant settings, regionalism focused on daily life and tangible details in an actual living environment. Regionalist writers tried to create a vivid sense of a time and place and experimented with dialect and slang in their narrations. Those writers also conjured up customs, conventional sayings and behaviors, as well as geography in their works. Some distinguishable features of regionalist writing include informal language of narration and description of minute details of nature. For example, *The Adventures of Huckleberry Finn* is considered the most representative of the narrator's informal language and depiction of nature, in this novel, the Mississippi River.

On the other hand, regionalism reflected Americans' new awareness after the Civil War that they formed a unified nation. Paradoxically, facing the political change, writers were eager to document traditional ways of life in response to readers' curiosity about regions that they had no opportunity to set foot on. Overall, readers can sense nostalgia in regionalist novels, for example, *The Adventures of Tom Sawyer* is a nostalgic novel of the experience of growing up in Missouri.

請聽與短文相關的課堂內容 ▶  *MP3 037*

Now listen to a lecture in an American literature class regarding the The Adventures of Huckleberry Finn

（將聽到的重點，列在下列筆記欄內，並於練習後將記下的重點與高分範文的摘要重點作對照檢視是否記憶到關鍵重點。）

_____

_____

_____

_____

_____

⏱ 寫作實測

（在閱讀與播放音檔後，實際演練於 20 分鐘內完成整合題寫作，於電腦上打字完成 150-225 字數的英文。完成試題後請詳讀高分範文檢視與範文間的差異，強化應考實力）

_____

_____

_____

_____

_____

整合能力強化① 訊息整合

比較「閱讀」和「聽力」講堂中內容的差異處，試著列出特點，比較特點後就能釐清主要差異或相似處，並著手開始寫作。

「閱讀」

- _____
- _____
- _____
- _____
- _____

「聽力」

- _____
- _____
- _____
- _____
- _____

整合訊息後，可以開始著手寫段落內容，寫完後可以與範文作對照。

- _____
- _____
- _____
- _____
- _____

Part 1
獨立篇

Part 2
整合篇

① 在 2010 年,美國人曾慶祝哈克歷險記出版 125 周年。

_____

_____

ANS:

In 2010, Americans celebrated the fact that *The Adventures of Huckleberry Finn* turned 125.

② 當馬克・吐溫在 1885 年出版此小說時,他大概沒預想到這本小說會成為美國文學的經典作品,而且是在許多國高中必讀的書。

_____

_____

ANS:

When Mark Twain published it in 1885, he probably did not envision that the novel would become an icon in American Literature, and a must-read in many middle and high schools in America.

③ 連艾尼斯・海明威都宣稱《哈克歷險記》是所有現代美國文學的開端。

_____

_____

ANS:

Even Earnest Hemingway claimed that *The Adventures of Huckleberry Finn* marked the beginning of all modern American literature.

④ 在過去幾年，這本小說的確因為用字引起激烈的爭議，尤其是「黑鬼」這個字，現在這個字是有貶抑和種族歧視意味的。

_____

_____

ANS:

Over the past few years, the novel did stir intense controversy for its word choices, especially the word "nigger", which is considered pejorative and racist today.

⑤ 然而，如果我們只依據用字就批評這本小說，我們會忽略馬克‧吐溫想要傳達的重要主題，及他協助塑造的文學傳統，就是我們所稱的區域主義。

_____

_____

ANS:

However, if we criticize the novel only based on word choices, we are missing the important theme that Mark Twain aimed to convey and the literary tradition that he helped to shape, a tradition we call regionalism.

⑥ 這本小說本質上是反對奴隸制度及反對種族主義的。我的意思是我們應該記住當時的歷史情境和區域性的影響。

_____

_____

ANS:

The novel is essentially anti-slavery and anti-racism. I mean, we should keep the historical context and regional influence in mind.

⑦ 這本小說的背景是設定在南北戰爭之前,當時「黑鬼」這個字普遍被使用,而且馬克・吐溫將哈克描寫成從一個功能失常的白人家庭被放逐的局外人。

_____

_____

ANS:

The novel was set in the pre-Civil War period, during which "nigger" was commonly used, and Mark Twain portrayed Huck as an outcast from a dysfunctional white family.

⑧ 哈克的語言充滿俚語和文法錯誤的句子,以一位在密蘇里州的聖彼得鎮成長的男孩角度敘述。聖彼得鎮鄰近密西西比河。

_____

_____

ANS:

Huck's language is full of slang and grammatically incorrect sentences, spoken from the perspectives of a young boy growing up in St. Petersburg, Missouri, a town on the Mississippi River.

⑨ 透過哈克充滿地方色彩的語言和他跟一位奴隸，吉姆，的友誼，
吐溫想批評的是當時的社會及種族不公不義的現象。

_____

_____

ANS:

Through the wit in Huck's colloquial language and his friendship with the slave, Jim, Twain wanted to criticize the social and racial injustice at that time.

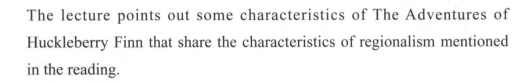

The lecture points out some characteristics of The Adventures of Huckleberry Finn that share the characteristics of regionalism mentioned in the reading.

課堂講述指出數個《哈克歷險記》的特色，跟閱讀篇章提到的區域主義特色是一樣的。

The first characteristic that the professor raised is the dialect and slang spoken by the characters. Mark Twain maintained the dialect used in the pre-Civil War period that forms the background of this novel. The professor used the example of the word "nigger", which is racist nowadays, yet before the Civil War, it was in common usage. In other words, it was a customary word during that period, reflecting one of the features, conventional sayings, given in the reading. Also, the novel was published after the Civil War, corresponding to the period of this literary style mentioned in the reading. The theme of the novel, that is, criticism of slavery, echoes one of the reasons that regionalism burgeoned as presented in the reading, the abolition of slavery.

教授提出的第一個特色是小說角色說的方言和俚語。這本小說的背景是南北戰爭之前的時期，馬克・吐溫保留當時的方言。教授舉的例子是「黑鬼」這個字，現在這個字有種族歧視的意味，但在南北戰爭之前是普遍被使用的。換言之，這是那時的慣用字，呼應閱讀提到的特色之一，即約定俗成的說法。另外，這本小說在南北戰爭後出版，符合閱讀篇章提及的此文學風格的時期。小說的主題，即對奴隸制度的批評，呼應了閱讀篇章指出的區域主義急速發展的理由，其中之一即廢除奴隸制度。

Furthermore, another regionalist characteristic of the novel is the detailed description of the Mississippi River, which is not really relevant to the major plot. By doing so, the novelist wanted readers to have a realistic sense of the local nature. The emphasis on nature is also included in the reading.

此外，小說裡另一個區域主義的特色是對密西西比河的詳細描述，不見得跟主要劇情有關。小說家藉此讓讀者對當地自然風景有寫實的感受。閱讀篇章也提及對自然風景的重視。

The characteristics summarized above demonstrate that the novel carries regionalist style.

以上總結的特色證明這本小說屬於區域主義風格。

關鍵句 ①

The lecture points out some characteristics of *The Adventures of Huckleberry Finn* that share the characteristics of regionalism mentioned in the reading.

解析

此句是整篇的主旨句（thesis statement），主旨句必須闡明閱讀篇章和聽力篇章主要論點彼此間的關係。不須發表個人意見。此單元題目屬於 support 類型，即閱讀和聽力篇章的主要論點互相支持，或一方提出理論，另一方提出佐證。

關鍵句 ②

Also, the novel was published after the Civil War, corresponding to the period of this literary style mentioned in the reading. The theme of the novel, that is, criticism of slavery, echoes one of the reasons that regionalism burgeoned as presented in the reading, the abolition of slavery.

解析

此句詳細整合閱讀篇章和聽力篇章互相呼應的重點，且運用分詞構句：S+V, corresponding to...及 N1 echoes N2, as presented in ... 。將立場相似的重點整合的動詞有（1）呼應：reflect, echo, correspond to（2）支持：support, fortify, buttress, enhance, ally with。

266

閱讀短文中譯

請總結課堂講述對《哈克歷險記》描述的重點特色，並解釋此小說為何被歸類於閱讀短文中描述的區域主義風格。

區域主義是一種十九世紀末期在美國流行的文學風格。有名的區域主義風格小說包括馬克‧吐溫的《哈克歷險記》，凱特‧蕭邦的《覺醒》，和艾蒂斯‧霍頓的《歡樂之屋》。此風格的起源也跟反對之前流行的浪漫主義有關，並力求呼應十九世紀美國在社會及政治上劇烈的變化，包括內戰結束、廢除奴隸制度及工業革命。

區域主義不像浪漫主義重視強烈情感和奢華的背景，反而重視日常生活及生活環境的具體細節。區域主義作家嘗試創造栩栩如生的時代感和地區感，且在敘述中嘗試使用方言和俚語。這些作家也在作品中融入習俗，約定俗成的語言或行為，和地理特色。一些可辨識區域風格文章的特色包含不正式的敘述語言及對大自然的瑣碎描述。例如，《哈克歷險記》被視為敘述者使用不正式語言和描繪大自然的最佳代表作品，這本小說裡，大自然主要指的是密西西比河。

另一方面，區域主義反映的是內戰結束後，美國人對他們是統一國家的新意識形態。矛盾地，作家面對這種政治變化，反而迫切地想要紀錄傳統生活方式，也因應讀者對那些未曾造訪之地的好奇心。大致而言，讀者讀區域風格小說能感受懷舊氛圍，例如《湯姆歷險記》是本描述在密蘇里州成長的懷舊風格小說。

Now listen to a lecture in an American literature class regarding The Adventures of Huckleberry Finn

現在請聽一篇與閱讀篇章一樣主題的課堂講述。

(Professor) In 2010, Americans celebrated the fact that The Adventures of Huckleberry Finn turned 125. When Mark Twain published it in 1885, he probably did not envision that the novel would become an icon in American Literature, and a must-read in many middle and high schools in America.

在 2010 年,美國人曾慶祝哈克歷險記出版 125 周年。當馬克・吐溫在 1885 年出版此小說時,他大概沒預想到這本小說會成為美國文學的經典作品,而且是在許多國高中必讀的書。

Even Earnest Hemingway claimed that The Adventures of Huckleberry Finn marked the beginning of all modern American literature. What makes this novel so quintessential in American literature?

連艾尼斯・海明威都宣稱《哈克歷險記》是所有現代美國文學的開端。是甚麼讓這本小說在美國文學深具代表性?

To begin with, what probably impressed readers the most is the dialect which is so different from the Standard English we are used to nowadays.

首先，讓讀者印象最深刻的是書中的方言，跟我們現在習慣的標準英文差異甚大。

Over the past few years, the novel did stir intense controversy for its word choices, especially the word "nigger", which is considered pejorative and racist today.

在過去幾年，這本小說的確因為用字引起激烈的爭議，尤其是「黑鬼」這個字，現在這個字是有貶抑和種族歧視意味的。

However, if we criticize the novel only based on word choices, we are missing the important theme that Mark Twain aimed to convey and the literary tradition that he helped to shape, a tradition we call regionalism.

然而，如果我們只依據用字就批評這本小說，我們會忽略馬克・吐溫想要傳達的重要主題，及他協助塑造的文學傳統，就是我們所稱的區域主義。

The novel is essentially antislavery and antiracism. I mean, we should keep the historical context and regional influence in mind. The novel was set in the pre-Civil War period, during which "nigger" was commonly

Part 1
獨立篇

Part 2
整合篇

269

used, and Mark Twain portrayed Huck as an outcast from a dysfunctional white family.

這本小說本質上是反對奴隸制度及反對種族主義的。我的意思是我們應該記住當時的歷史情境和區域性的影響。這本小說的背景是設定在南北戰爭之前，當時「黑鬼」這個字普遍被使用，而且馬克・吐溫將哈克描寫成從一個功能失常的白人家庭被放逐的局外人。

Huck's language is full of slang and grammatically incorrect sentences, spoken from the perspectives of a young boy growing up in St. Petersburg, Missouri, a town on the Mississippi River. Through the wit in Huck's colloquial language and his friendship with the slave, Jim, Twain wanted to criticize the social and racial injustice at that time.

哈克的語言充滿俚語和文法錯誤的句子，以一位在密蘇里州的聖彼得鎮成長的男孩角度敘述。聖彼得鎮鄰近密西西比河。透過哈克充滿地方色彩的語言和他跟一位奴隸，吉姆，的友誼，吐溫想批評的是當時的社會及種族不公不義的現象。

Another important element in the novel that echoes the tradition of regionalism is the Mississippi River. Regionalist writers had the tendency to elaborate on actual geographical details which might not be directly related to the plot.

Part 1
獨立篇

另一個呼應地區主義的重要元素是密西西比河。區域主義作家傾向詳細地描繪實際的地理細節，而這些細節可能跟劇情沒有直接連結。

Part 2
整合篇

Twain often digressed from the plot to describe the details of the Mississippi River, allowing readers to sense its majestic view.

吐溫常常偏離劇情去描述此河的細節，讓讀者感受到壯觀的景象。

UNIT 06

美國文學類：
烏托邦文學及反烏托邦文學
Utopia and Dystopia

📖 *INSTRUCTIONS*

You have *20 minutes* to plan and write your response. Your response will be judged on the basis of the quality of your writing and on how well your response presents the points in the lecture and their relationships to the reading passage. Typically, an effective response will be 150 to 225 words.

Summarize the points made in the lecture you just heard, explaining how they cast doubt on points made in the reading.

Reading time: 3 minutes

Summarize the main points in the reading and the lecture, explaining how they contrast one another.

The word "utopia" derived its origin from Sir Thomas More's novel,

Utopia, written in Latin in 1516 and translated into English in 1551. More made up this word by combining the Greek words "outopos", meaning "no place" and "eutopos", meaning "good place". Although nowadays the word generally means a perfect world, some experts argue that the connotation arose from a misunderstanding about More's original intention. More intended to emphasize fictionality, and thus the title simply meant "no place".

Despite various interpretations, most agree that utopia implies a perfect world which is unattainable, ironically a nowhere place. A much earlier example of utopia is Plato's *The Republic*, in which Plato depicted an ideal society reigned by philosopher-kings. The idea of utopia continued in the 18th and 19th centuries; for example, utopian traits were illustrated in Jonathan Swift's *Gulliver's Travels* and Samuel Butler's *Erewhon*, which is an anagram of the word "nowhere".

What are the characteristics of utopia? In More's book, he described a society with economic prosperity, a peaceful government and egalitarianism for civilians, which are the most obvious traits utopian fictions share. Moreover, technologies are applied to improve human living conditions; independent thought and free flow of information are encouraged. Although the government exists, citizens are united by a set of central ideas, while abiding by moral codes. The term government in a utopia state is very different from our idea of government in the present reality. The government in a utopia is loosely composed of citizenry, without a complicated hierarchy. Furthermore, people revere nature and reverse the damage to ecology due to industrialization.

請聽與短文相關的課堂內容 ▶ *MP3 039*

Now listen to a lecture in a literature class regarding dystopia

（將聽到的重點，列在下列筆記欄內，並於練習後將記下的重點與高分範文的摘要重點作對照檢視是否記憶到關鍵重點。）

_____

_____

_____

_____

寫作實測

（在閱讀與播放音檔後，實際演練於 20 分鐘內完成整合題寫作，於電腦上打字完成 150-225 字數的英文。完成試題後請詳讀高分範文檢視與範文間的差異，強化應考實力）

_____

_____

_____

_____

整合能力強化① 訊息整合

比較「閱讀」和「聽力」講堂中內容的差異處，試著列出特點，比較特點後就能釐清主要差異或相似處，並著手開始寫作。

「閱讀」

- _____
- _____
- _____
- _____
- _____

「聽力」

- _____
- _____
- _____
- _____
- _____

整合訊息後，可以開始著手寫段落內容，寫完後可以與範文作對照。

- _____
- _____
- _____
- _____
- _____

① 在今日的流行文化中,反烏托邦的概念在青少年小說和好萊塢電影中越來越受歡迎,如同《飢餓遊戲》的小說和電影之成功已經證明了。

_____

_____

ANS:

In today's popular culture, the idea of dystopia is gaining more popularity in young adult fiction and Hollywood movies, as the success of the novels and movies of *The Hunger Games* series has demonstrated.

② 你們可能從字首 dys-就知道反烏托邦的意思,它暗示的是情況跟烏托邦相反的負面地方。

_____

_____

ANS:

You might know the meaning of dystopia simply from the prefix dys-, implying a negative place with conditions opposite to utopia.

③ 事實上,我們能追溯反烏托邦文學的起源至 1605 年,是一本名為 *Mundus Alter et Idem* 的拉丁文諷刺小說,書名的意思是「一個舊世界和新世界」,作者是約瑟夫・霍爾,他是英國諾威治的主

Part 1
獨立篇

Part 2
整合篇

教。

_____

_____

ANS:

In fact, we can trace the origin of dystopian literature way back to 1605, to a satire in Latin called *Mundus Alter et Idem*, meaning "an old world and a new", written by Joseph Hall, Bishop of Norwich, England.

④ 《一個舊世界和新世界》嘲諷倫敦的生活型態及羅馬天主教的習俗。

_____

_____

ANS:

An Old World and a New satirizes life in London and customs of the Roman Catholic Church.

⑤ 這本書也啟發了強納森・斯威夫特的《格列佛遊記》。

_____

_____

ANS:

It also served as an inspiration to Jonathan Swift's *Gulliver's Travels*.

⑥ 提到強納森‧斯威夫特的《格列佛遊記》，你們有些人可能把它視為烏托邦小說。

_____

_____

ANS:

Speaking of Jonathan Swift's *Gulliver's Travels*, some of you might consider it utopian fiction.

⑦ 或者反烏托邦可能表面上假裝成烏托邦，形成一種模糊的文學類型。

_____

_____

ANS:

Or a dystopia might be disguised as a utopia, forming an ambiguous genre.

⑧ 一例是在山謬‧巴特勒的《烏有之鄉》裡，兩個種類的特色都並存。

_____

_____

ANS:

One example is Samuel Butler's *Erewhon*, which consists of utopian and dystopian traits.

⑨ 二十世紀最有名的反烏托邦小說應該是艾爾道斯‧赫胥黎 1931 年的著作《美麗新世界》和喬治‧歐威爾 1949 年的著作《1984》

_____

_____

ANS:

In the 20th century, the most famous dystopian works of fiction are probably Aldous Huxley's *Brave New World*, written in 1931 and George Orwell's *1984*, written in 1949.

The reading and lecture delineate the contrary styles of utopian and dystopian literature by depicting the representative works and various traits of both literary genres.

閱讀篇章及課堂講述藉由描寫烏托邦及反烏托邦兩種文學類型的代表作品和其特色，勾勒出兩種相反的風格。

First, the reading and the lecture explain the opposite definitions of these two words. Whereas utopia is a deliberately invented word with its origins in Greek, meaning an ideal place or a place that doesn't exist, a dystopia is an atrocious place contrary to a utopia.

首先，閱讀篇章及課堂講述解釋這兩個字的相反定義。烏托邦是一個刻意被創造出的字，源自希臘文，意為理想的地方或不存在之地，相反地，反烏托邦是個險惡之地。

Next, the reading traces back to the earliest utopian fiction, Plato's The Republic and gives the utopian examples from British literature, which are Jonathan Swift's Gulliver's Travels and Samuel Butler's Erewhon, while the lecture points out that the boundary between utopian and dystopian literature is sometimes not so definite, as both styles are present in the latter two works of fiction.

其次，閱讀篇章追溯至最初的烏托邦小說， 柏拉圖的《共和國》，並提出英國文學的作品為例，即強納森・斯威夫特的《格列佛遊記》和山謬・巴特勒的《烏有之鄉》，而課堂講述指出烏托邦和反烏托邦的界線有時候並非絕對，就如同兩種風格在後者兩本小說中都有出現。

Third, in contrast to the features of a utopia, such as encouragement of independent thoughts, equal status for all citizens, and a government without obvious hierarchy, the features of a dystopia include the government's dictatorial oppression of citizens, lack of equality, and abolishment of individual freedoms.

第三，反烏托邦的特色包含政府對公民的獨裁壓迫，缺乏平等及剝奪個人自由，這些與烏托邦的特色相反，如鼓勵獨立思考、公民均享平等，及沒有明顯階級的政府。

In conclusion, the dissimilar characteristics of utopia and dystopia are discussed supported by the renowned works from both genres.

總而言之，烏托邦和反烏托邦的差異特色皆被討論，並以兩種文學類型的知名作品作為佐證。

關鍵句 ①

Next, the reading traces back to the earliest utopian fiction, Plato's *The Republic*, and gives the utopian examples from British literature, which are Jonathan Swift's *Gulliver's Travels* and Samuel Butler's *Erewhon*, while the lecture points out that the boundary between utopian and dystopian literature is sometimes not so definite, as both styles are present in the latter two works of fiction.

解析

以從屬連接詞 while 連接兩個意義相反或落差甚大的子句,而 while 前後兩個子句又各包含兩個小子句,分別由 and 及 as 連接。

關鍵句 ②

In conclusion, the dissimilar characteristics of utopia and dystopia are discussed, supported by the renowned works from both genres.

解析

句尾的分詞片語 supported by ... 是由形容詞子句簡化而來,原本的完整子句:which are supported by ... ,省略 which are,保留過去分詞 supported。

閱讀短文中譯

請總結閱讀短文和課堂講述的重點，並解釋它們如何互相駁斥。

烏托邦一詞的來源是湯瑪士・摩爾在 1516 年以拉丁文寫的小說《烏托邦》，此著作在 1551 年被翻譯成英文。摩爾將希臘文的 "outopos"（意為「不存在之地」）和 "eutopos"（意為「好地方」）合併，創造出這詞。雖然現在這詞通常指的是完美世界，有些專家主張這涵義是誤解了摩爾的原意。摩爾原本是著重在虛構性，因此書名只是單純表達「不存在之地」。

儘管有不同的詮釋，大部份的專家同意烏托邦暗喻的是一個不可能達到的完美世界，諷刺地也就是一個「不存在之地」。更早期的烏托邦例子是柏拉圖的《共和國》，柏拉圖描繪了一個由哲學家國王統治的理想社會。烏托邦的概念延續到十八和十九世紀；例如，強納森・斯威夫特的《格列佛遊記》和山謬・巴特勒的《烏有之鄉》都描繪了烏托邦特色，《烏有之鄉》這個字是「不存在之地」的顛倒重組字。

烏托邦的特色為何？在摩爾的書裡，他描述一個擁有繁榮經濟，祥和政府和公民平等的社會，這些是烏托邦小說共有的最明顯的特色。此外，科技被應用來改善人類的生活狀態，獨立的思考和資訊自由流通是被鼓勵的。雖然政府存在，公民是被一組中心思想所團結，同時他們遵守道德規範。烏托邦的政府一詞跟我們現在對政府的概念非常不同。烏托邦政府是由公民團體鬆散地組織而成，沒有複雜的階級制度。而且，人們尊敬大自然並反轉了工業化對生態造成的損害。

Now listen to a lecture in a literature class regarding dystopia

現在請聽一篇關於反烏托邦的文學課堂講述。

(Professor) In today's popular culture, the idea of dystopia is gaining more popularity in young adult fiction and Hollywood movies, as the success of the novels and movies of *The Hunger Games* series has demonstrated. You might know the meaning of dystopia simply from the prefix dys-, implying a negative place with conditions opposite to utopia.

在今日的流行文化中,反烏托邦的概念在青少年小說和好萊塢電影中越來越受歡迎,如同《飢餓遊戲》的小說和電影之成功已經證明了。你們可能從字首 dys- 就知道反烏托邦的意思,它暗示的是情況跟烏托邦相反的負面地方。

In fact, we can trace the origin of dystopian literature way back to 1605, to a satire in Latin called *Mundus Alter et Idem*, meaning "an old world and a new", written by Joseph Hall, Bishop of Norwich, England. *An Old World and a New* satirizes life in London and customs of the Roman Catholic Church. It also served as an inspiration to Jonathan Swift's *Gulliver's Travels*.

事實上，我們能追溯反烏托邦文學的起源至 1605 年，是一本名為 *Mundus Alter et Idem* 的拉丁文諷刺小說，書名的意思是「一個舊世界和新世界」，作者是約瑟夫・霍爾，他是英國諾威治的主教。《一個舊世界和新世界》嘲諷倫敦的生活型態及羅馬天主教的習俗。這本書也啟發了強納森・斯威夫特的《格列佛遊記》。

Speaking of Jonathan Swift's *Gulliver's Travels*, some of you might consider it utopian fiction.

提到強納森・斯威夫特的《格列佛遊記》，你們有些人可能把它視為烏托邦小說。嗯，它是烏托邦，也是反烏托邦小說。

Well, it is both utopian and dystopian. *Gulliver's Travels* illustrates utopian and dystopian places. Or a dystopia might be covered as a utopia, forming an ambiguous genre. One example is Samuel Butler's *Erewhon*, which consists of utopian and dystopian traits.

烏托邦和反烏托邦地區《格列佛遊記》都描述了。或者反烏托邦可能表面上假裝成烏托邦，形成一種模糊的文學類型。一例是在山謬・巴特勒的《烏有之鄉》裡，兩個種類的特色都並存。

In the 20th century, the most famous dystopian works of fiction are probably Aldous Huxley's *Brave New World*, written in 1931 and George Orwell's *1984*, written in 1949.

二十世紀最有名的反烏托邦小說應該是艾爾道斯‧赫胥黎 1931 年的著作《美麗新世界》和喬治‧歐威爾 1949 年的著作《1984》。

It is not hard to understand that the characteristics of dystopia contribute to its popularity in popular fiction and movies. Those characteristics tend to create tension and anxiety, factors that draw contemporary audience. Those include totalitarian control of citizens, a bureaucratic government, restriction of freedom and information, as well as constant surveillance on civilians with technology.

不難理解，反烏托邦的特色導致了這個概念在流行小說和電影中非常普遍。那些特色會創造緊繃和焦慮感，這些都是吸引當代觀眾的因素。特色包括對公民的獨裁控制，官僚化政府，對自由和資訊的限制，及不斷用科技監視人民。

Civilians' individuality and equality are abolished, while a central figurehead or bureaucracy exerts dictatorial control over society. Other traits are associated with doomsday, such as poverty, hunger, and the destruction of nature.

人民的個人特色和平等權被剝奪了，而一位中央領導或官僚體系以獨裁方式控制社會。其他特色跟末日有關聯，例如貧窮、飢餓和對大自然的破壞。

NOTE

西洋藝術類：
塗鴉藝術及凱斯・哈林
Graffiti Art and Keith Haring

📖 INSTRUCTIONS

You have *20 minutes* to plan and write your response. Your response will be judged on the basis of the quality of your writing and on how well your response presents the points in the lecture and their relationships to the reading passage. Typically, an effective response will be 150 to 225 words.

Summarize the points made in the lecture you just heard, explaining how they cast doubt on points made in the reading.

Reading time: 3 minutes

Summarize the main points in the lecture and Keith Haring's contributions, as described in the reading.

Keith Haring has become a worldwide icon of the 20th century Pop Art.

His contribution is multifaceted, from changing our idea of street art to incorporating social and political messages in Pop Art.

In Haring's early career in the 1980s, he was fined numerous times for his graffiti drawings in the New York subway system since the police viewed his art as vandalism. Notwithstanding, Haring considered subway drawings his responsibility of communicating art to the public. While he was drawing on the blank panels, he was often surrounded and observed by commuters. Being a prolific artist, he could produce about 40 drawings a day. Yet, most of his subway drawings were not recorded, as they were either cleaned or covered by new advertisements. It was the ephemeral nature that acted as an impetus for him to reinvent themes with easily identifiable images, such as babies, dogs, and angels, all illustrated with outlines. His themes involve sexuality, war, birth, and death, often mocking the mainstream society in caricatures.

As Haring's reputation grew, he took on larger projects. His most notable work is the public mural titled, "Crack is Wack", inspired by his studio assistant who was addicted to crack and addressing the deteriorating drug issue in New York. The mural is representative of Haring's broad concerns for the American society in the 1980s. He was a social activist as well, heavily involved in socio-political movements, in which he participated in charitable support for children and fought against racial discrimination. Before his death at age 31, he established the Keith Haring Foundation and the Pop Shop; both have continued his legacy till today.

Now listen to a lecture in an art class regarding graffiti

（將聽到的重點，列在下列筆記欄內，並於練習後將記下的重點與高分範文的摘要重點作對照檢視是否記憶到關鍵重點。）

_____

_____

_____

_____

 寫作實測

（在閱讀與播放音檔後，實際演練於 20 分鐘內完成整合題寫作，於電腦上打字完成 150-225 字數的英文。完成試題後請詳讀高分範文檢視與範文間的差異，強化應考實力）

_____

_____

_____

_____

整合能力強化① 訊息整合

比較「閱讀」和「聽力」講堂中內容的差異處，試著列出特點，比較特點後就能釐清主要差異或相似處，並著手開始寫作。

「閱讀」

- _____
- _____
- _____
- _____
- _____

「聽力」

- _____
- _____
- _____
- _____
- _____

整合訊息後，可以開始著手寫段落內容，寫完後可以與範文作對照。

- _____
- _____
- _____
- _____
- _____

① 塗鴉的歷史就跟文字的歷史一樣久,塗鴉的例子可追溯到古希臘、古埃及和羅馬帝國。

_____

_____

ANS:

Graffiti has existed for as long as written words have existed, with examples traced back to Ancient Greece, Ancient Egypt, and the Roman Empire.

② 事實上,graffiti 這個字發源自羅馬帝國。有些人甚至將新石器時代的穴居人所畫的洞穴壁畫視為塗鴉最早的形式,使得塗鴉成為現存最久的藝術。

_____

_____

ANS:

In fact, the word graffiti came from the Roman Empire. Some even consider cave drawings by cavemen in the Neolithic Age the earliest form of graffiti, and thus make it the longest existent art form.

③ 基本上,塗鴉指的是未經法律許可在公共領域的壁面上潦草書寫,畫畫或噴漆形成的文字或圖案。

_____

_____

ANS:

Basically, graffiti refers to writing or drawings that have been scrawled, painted, or sprayed on surfaces in public in an illicit manner.

④ 塗鴉的主要功能包括表達個人情緒，記錄歷史事件，及傳達政治訊息。

_____

_____

ANS:

The general functions of graffiti include expressing personal emotions, recording historical events, and conveying political messages.

⑤ 然而，今日塗鴉已經在主流藝術中取得一席之地，而且對許多塗鴉藝術家而言，他們的作品已經被高度商業化並帶來高度利潤。

_____

_____

ANS:

Nevertheless, today graffiti has found its place in mainstream art, and for many graffiti artists, their works have become highly commercialized and lucrative.

⑥ 當今的藝術性塗鴉是在過去二十五年間於紐約市中心興起的，當時街頭藝術家未經法律許可就在公共建築、馬路上的標誌或公共運輸工具上面畫畫及寫字，比較普遍的是畫在地鐵車廂的外層。

_____

_____

ANS:

Contemporary artistic graffiti has just arisen in the past twenty five years in the inner city of New York, with street artists painting and writing illegitimately on public buildings, street signs or public transportation, more commonly on the exteriors of subway trains.

⑦ 這些藝術家實驗不同的風格和媒介，例如噴漆和金屬模板。

_____

_____

ANS:

These artists experimented with different styles and mediums, such as sprays and stencils.

⑧ 藝術性塗鴉和傳統塗鴉的差異，在於前者已從在牆壁上潦草畫畫進化成表達個人和政治意涵的複雜及高技術的型式。

_____

_____

ANS:

The difference between artistic graffiti and traditional graffiti is that the former has evolved from scribbling on a wall to a complex and skillful form of personal and political expression.

⑨ 塗鴉藝術家也和流行服飾設計師合作拓展出許多產品，提高此藝術在日常生活和全球的能見度。

_____

_____

ANS:

Graffiti artists have also branched out to collaborate with fashion designers and produce numerous products, increasing the daily and global presence of this art form.

The lecture outlines the history of graffiti from its earliest origin to its recent development in the U.S., while the reading focuses on Keith Haring's artworks and his contributions.

課堂講述勾勒塗鴉的歷史，從最早的起源至近期在美國的發展，而閱讀篇章著重凱斯・哈林的作品和貢獻。

The lecture first points out that the history of graffiti is as long as that of written words, which can be exemplified by the origin of the word graffiti from the Roman Empire. Another view even holds that graffiti might be dated back to the Neolithic Age, to cave drawings. Then the lecture shifts to artistic graffiti which developed in New York City in the past 25 years, offering details such as locations and mediums. Besides, it describes graffiti artists that have turned their careers to the fashion industry, allowing consumers to attain their works in commercialized forms. Finally, Keith Haring's Pop Shop is raised to fortify the aforementioned description.

課堂講述首先指出塗鴉的歷史跟文字歷史一樣久，並以塗鴉這個字發源於羅馬帝國為例。另一個看法甚至認為塗鴉可追溯到新石器時代的洞穴繪畫。接著講述轉而描述在紐約市過去 25 年間發展出的藝術性塗鴉，並提出塗鴉地點和媒介等細節。此外，講述提及塗鴉藝術家將職業轉向至流行產業，讓消費者可以透過商業型式取得他們的作品。最後，講述提出凱斯・哈林的流行商店以加強之前的敘述。

The reading not only depicts Keith Haring's major artworks, but also mentions his diverse contribution to the American society. In his early career, he was known for subway drawings, and another renowned work is a public mural that conveys an anti-drug message. His other contributions included charities for children and anti-racism campaigns.

閱讀篇章不但描述凱斯‧哈林的作品，也提到他對美國社會多方面的貢獻。在他早期的職涯，他以地鐵繪畫聞名，而另一個知名作品是一幅傳達反對毒品訊息的公共壁畫。他其他的貢獻包括兒童慈善和反對種族歧視的活動。

關鍵句 ①

The lecture first points out that the history of graffiti is as long as that of written words, which can be exemplified by the origin of the word graffiti from the Roman Empire.

解析

主要動詞 point out 的受詞是 that 引導的名詞子句。名詞子句互相比較兩個事物的歷史，as long as 之後的代名詞 that 是代替 history，注意代名詞 that 不可省略。形容詞子句 which ...，關係代名詞 which 的先行詞是 that 引導的名詞子句。

關鍵句 ②

Besides, it describes graffiti artists that have turned their careers to the fashion industry, allowing consumers to attain their works in commercialized forms.

解析

動詞 describe 的受詞是 graffiti artists。graffiti artists 由關係代名詞的 that 導引的限定形容詞子句修飾。分詞片語 allowing... 是由形容詞子句 which allows... 簡化而來。

閱讀短文中譯

請總結課堂講述的重點及閱讀短文描述的凱斯・哈林的貢獻。

凱斯・哈林已成為二十世紀流行藝術的代表人物。他的貢獻是多方面的，從改變我們對街頭藝術的觀念到將社會及政治訊息融入流行藝術。

在 1980 年代哈林早期的職涯裡，他因為在紐約市地鐵系統塗鴉被罰款許多次，因為警察將他的藝術視為破壞公物。然而，哈林認為地鐵繪畫是他的責任，藉此他能將藝術溝通給大眾。當他在空白的長板子上繪畫時，他常常被通勤者圍觀。身為多產的藝術家，他一天可以畫大約四十幅塗鴉。但是，他大部份的地鐵繪畫沒有被記錄下來，因為它們不是被清潔掉，就是被新的廣告蓋上。正是這種稍縱即逝的本質形成他不斷重新創作主題的動力。他的塗鴉主題運用容易辨識的圖案，例如嬰兒、小狗和天使形象，而所有的圖案都只有外觀輪廓。他的主題牽涉了性意識、戰爭、出生及死亡，且經常以諷刺漫畫嘲諷主流社會。

隨著哈林的名聲提高，他進行更大型的計畫。他最值得一提的作品是名為「吸毒等同發瘋」公共壁畫，這幅壁畫的靈感來自他對毒品上癮的工作室助理，同時也針對紐約市日益惡化的毒品問題。這幅壁畫代表了哈林對 1980 年代美國社會的廣泛關注。他也是位行動主義者，深度參與社會及政治方面的活動，並支援兒童慈善活動及反對種族歧視。在他 31 歲過世前，他創立了凱斯・哈林基金會及流行商店，至今兩者都持續的推廣他留下的文化遺產。

Now listen to a lecture in an art class regarding graffiti

現在請聽一篇關於塗鴉藝術的藝術課堂講述。

(Professor) Graffiti has existed for as long as written words have existed, with examples traced back to Ancient Greece, Ancient Egypt, and the Roman Empire.

塗鴉的歷史就跟文字的歷史一樣久，塗鴉的例子可追溯到古希臘、古埃及和羅馬帝國。

In fact, the word graffiti came from the Roman Empire. Some even consider cave drawings by cavemen in the Neolithic Age the earliest form of graffiti, and thus make it the longest existent art form.

事實上，graffiti 這個字發源自羅馬帝國。有些人甚至將新石器時代的穴居人所畫的洞穴壁畫視為塗鴉最早的形式，使得塗鴉成為現存最久的藝術。

Basically, graffiti refers to writing or drawings that have been scrawled, painted, or sprayed on surfaces in public in an illicit manner. The general functions of graffiti include expressing personal emotions, recording

300

historical events, and conveying political messages.

基本上，塗鴉指的是未經法律許可在公共領域的壁面上潦草書寫，畫畫或噴漆形成的文字或圖案。塗鴉的主要功能包括表達個人情緒，記錄歷史事件，及傳達政治訊息。

Nevertheless, today graffiti has found its place in mainstream art, and for many graffiti artists, their works have become highly commercialized and lucrative.

然而，今日塗鴉已經在主流藝術中取得一席之地，而且對許多塗鴉藝術家而言，他們的作品已經被高度商業化並帶來高度利潤。

Contemporary artistic graffiti has just arisen in the past twenty five years in the inner city of New York, with street artists painting and writing illegitimately on public buildings, street signs or public transportation, more commonly on the exteriors of subway trains.

當今的藝術性塗鴉是在過去二十五年間於紐約市中心興起的，當時街頭藝術家未經法律許可就在公共建築、馬路上的標誌或公共運輸工具上面畫畫及寫字，比較普遍的是畫在地鐵車廂的外層。

These artists experimented with different styles and mediums, such as sprays and stencils. The difference between artistic graffiti and traditional graffiti is that the former has evolved from scribbling on a wall to a complex and skillful form of personal and political expression.

這些藝術家實驗不同的風格和媒介，例如噴漆和金屬模板。藝術性塗鴉和傳統塗鴉的差異在於前者已從在牆壁上潦草畫畫進化成表達個人和政治意涵的複雜及高技術的型式。

Graffiti artists have also branched out to collaborate with fashion designers and produce numerous products, increasing the daily and global presence of this art form.

塗鴉藝術家也和流行服飾設計師合作拓展出許多產品，提高此藝術在日常生活和全球的能見度。

In the U. S., many graffiti artists have extended their careers to skateboard, apparel, and shoe design for companies such as DC Shoes, Adidas, and Osiris. The most famous American graffiti artist is probably Keith Haring, who brought his art into the commercial mainstream by opening his Pop Shop in New York in 1986, where the public could purchase commodities with Haring's graffiti imageries.

在美國，許多塗鴉藝術家已經將職涯延伸到滑板、服裝及鞋子設計，他們替 DC Shoes、愛迪達和 Osiris 等品牌設計。最有名的美國塗鴉藝術家可能是凱斯‧哈林。他在 1986 年於紐約開了他的普普店，將他的藝術帶入商業主流。在這間店大眾可以買到印有哈林的塗鴉圖案的商品。

Keith Haring viewed his Pop Shop as an extension of his subway drawings, with his philosophy of making art accessible to the public, not just to collectors.

哈林視流行商店為他的地鐵繪畫的延伸，這間店蘊含他對藝術的哲學，即藝術應該讓大眾輕易取得，而不是只針對收藏家。

UNIT 08

西洋藝術類：
現代主義建築及貝聿銘

Modern Architecture and I. M. Pei

INSTRUCTIONS

You have **20 minutes** to plan and write your response. Your response will be judged on the basis of the quality of your writing and on how well your response presents the points in the lecture and their relationships to the reading passage. Typically, an effective response will be 150 to 225 words.

Summarize the points made in the lecture you just heard, explaining how they cast doubt on points made in the reading.

Reading time: 3 minutes

Summarize the main points in the reading and listening, with an emphasis on the features of I. M. Pei's architectures.

"Modern architecture" is an overarching term, which generally is applied

304

to architectures emerging at the end of the 19th century under the influence of modernism and to those that shared similar characteristics throughout the 20th century. Compared with previous architectures, modern architectures focus more on geometric forms, harmony with location, and function over ornament.

Modern architectures exhibit certain characteristics, including simplicity in design, merging of nature and buildings, rectangular forms and linear structures. In the U.S., the most quintessential buildings are those designed by Frank Lloyd Wright, such as the Robie House and Fallingwater. Frank Lloyd Wright was referred to as "the greatest American architect of all time" by the American Institute of Architects, for he cultivated the original American architectural philosophy called "organic architecture", which means that architectures should be incorporated into their natural environment. Wright's buildings are characterized by linear elements. Numerous components, such as beams, posts, staircases and windows, are utilized to construct a linear space. The interior space also extends to the exterior, forming another feature, that is, blurring the boundary between indoor space and outdoor space. To achieve that, floor-to-ceiling glass windows are employed. Large expanses of glass not only bring in natural light, but also generate a magnificent view. Another iconic example that demonstrates the dramatic function of glass windows is the glass pyramid designed by I. M. Pei at the Louvre Museum in Paris.

In the 1960s, waves of criticism arose in reaction to modern architecture, and since the 1960s, the mainstream architectural philosophy has embraced postmodernism, gradually replacing modernism.

Now listen to a lecture in an art class regarding I. M. Pei, a renowned Chinese-American architect

（將聽到的重點，列在下列筆記欄內，並於練習後將記下的重點與高分範文的摘要重點作對照檢視是否記憶到關鍵重點。）

_____

_____

_____

_____

_____

寫作實測

（在閱讀與播放音檔後，實際演練於 20 分鐘內完成整合題寫作，於電腦上打字完成 150-225 字數的英文。完成試題後請詳讀高分範文檢視與範文間的差異，強化應考實力）

_____

_____

_____

_____

_____

整合能力強化① 訊息整合

比較「閱讀」和「聽力」講堂中內容的差異處，試著列出特點，比較特點後就能釐清主要差異或相似處，並著手開始寫作。

「閱讀」

- ＿＿＿＿＿＿＿＿＿＿＿＿＿＿＿＿＿＿＿＿＿＿＿＿＿
- ＿＿＿＿＿＿＿＿＿＿＿＿＿＿＿＿＿＿＿＿＿＿＿＿＿
- ＿＿＿＿＿＿＿＿＿＿＿＿＿＿＿＿＿＿＿＿＿＿＿＿＿
- ＿＿＿＿＿＿＿＿＿＿＿＿＿＿＿＿＿＿＿＿＿＿＿＿＿
- ＿＿＿＿＿＿＿＿＿＿＿＿＿＿＿＿＿＿＿＿＿＿＿＿＿

「聽力」

- ＿＿＿＿＿＿＿＿＿＿＿＿＿＿＿＿＿＿＿＿＿＿＿＿＿
- ＿＿＿＿＿＿＿＿＿＿＿＿＿＿＿＿＿＿＿＿＿＿＿＿＿
- ＿＿＿＿＿＿＿＿＿＿＿＿＿＿＿＿＿＿＿＿＿＿＿＿＿
- ＿＿＿＿＿＿＿＿＿＿＿＿＿＿＿＿＿＿＿＿＿＿＿＿＿
- ＿＿＿＿＿＿＿＿＿＿＿＿＿＿＿＿＿＿＿＿＿＿＿＿＿

整合訊息後，可以開始著手寫段落內容，寫完後可以與範文作對照。

- ＿＿＿＿＿＿＿＿＿＿＿＿＿＿＿＿＿＿＿＿＿＿＿＿＿
- ＿＿＿＿＿＿＿＿＿＿＿＿＿＿＿＿＿＿＿＿＿＿＿＿＿
- ＿＿＿＿＿＿＿＿＿＿＿＿＿＿＿＿＿＿＿＿＿＿＿＿＿
- ＿＿＿＿＿＿＿＿＿＿＿＿＿＿＿＿＿＿＿＿＿＿＿＿＿
- ＿＿＿＿＿＿＿＿＿＿＿＿＿＿＿＿＿＿＿＿＿＿＿＿＿

① 貝聿銘從在上海就讀高中快畢業時,他決定到美國念大學。他曾承認這個決定是受到賓‧克洛斯比的電影影響,在那些電影裡,美國的大學生活似乎是充滿了歡樂。

_____

_____

ANS:

As Pei's secondary education in Shanghai drew near an end, he decided to enter an American university, a decision which he once admitted was made under the influence of Bing Crosby movies, in which college life in America seemed full of fun.

② 雖然他很快就發現嚴格的學術生活和電影的描繪相差甚多,他就讀於麻省理工學院建築系時表現得非常優秀。

_____

_____

ANS:

Though he soon found out that the rigorous academic life differed drastically from the portrayal in movies, he excelled in the architecture school of the Massachusetts Institute of Technology (MIT).

③ 他尤其被現代建築吸引,現代建築的特色是極簡風和運用玻璃及鋼鐵素材,也是被法蘭克‧洛伊‧萊特影響。

Part 1
獨立篇

Part 2
整合篇

ANS:

Particularly, he was drawn to the school of modern architecture, featuring simplicity and the utilization of glass and steel materials, and influenced by architect Frank Lloyd Wright.

④ 在他的職業生涯中，貝聿銘設計了許多值得一提的建築。

ANS:

Throughout his career, Pei has designed numerous notable buildings.

⑤ 麥莎實驗室大樓展現了類似有機建築的哲學。

ANS:

The Mesa Laboratory embodied his philosophy akin to Organic Architecture.

⑥ 這棟建築物和諧地和洛磯山脈並存，看起來像是直接從岩石雕鑿出來的。

ANS:

The building rests harmoniously in the Rocky Mountains, as if sculpted out of rocks.

⑦ 之後，在 1963 年甘迺迪總統被刺殺後，甘迺迪夫人選擇貝聿銘為甘迺迪總統圖書館及紀念館做設計。此圖書館及紀念館包含一大片被玻璃環繞的方形中庭、三角錐狀的高塔和圓形的走道。

_____

_____

ANS:

Then, after President John F. Kennedy's assassination in 1963, Pei was chosen by Ms. Kennedy to design the John F. Kennedy Presidential Library and Museum, which includes a large square glass-enclosed courtyard with a triangular tower and a circular walkway.

⑧ 貝聿銘於 1980 年代執行了職業生涯中最具挑戰性的案子，就是巴黎羅浮宮博物館的翻新工程。

_____

_____

ANS:

Pei executed the most challenging project in his career in the 1980s, the renovation of the Louvre Museum in Paris.

⑨ 他決定在羅浮宮中庭的中央建造一座巨型玻璃和鋼鐵金字塔，這個決定最初引起爭議，但是玻璃金字塔完成後，它成為巴黎知名

的地標，也是貝聿銘最具代表性的作品。

_____

_____

ANS:

His decision to build a huge glass and steel pyramid at the center of the courtyard initially ignited controversy, yet since its completion, the glass pyramid has become a famous landmark in Paris and Pei's most representative work.

The reading passage depicts the school of modern architecture, with a focus on its development in the U.S., and the listening passage features I.M. Pei, the master of modern architecture.

閱讀篇章描述現代建築學派，特別是這個學派在美國的發展，而聽力篇章著重現代建築大師，貝聿銘。

Modern architecture is a comprehensive genre that includes architecture influenced by modernism, with traits such as functionality, simplicity, geometric shapes, and a harmonious relationship with the surrounding environment. The most representative architect of this genre is Frank Lloyd Wright, whose school is termed organic architecture. Organic architecture is characterized by linear design, lack of the definite boundary between interior and exterior and huge glass windows.

現代建築是一個廣泛的類型，包括被現代主義影響的建築，這個類型的特色有功能性、極簡風、幾何形狀和建築與周遭環境的和諧關係。此類型最具代表性的建築師是法蘭克‧洛伊‧萊特，他的學派被稱為有機建築。有機建築的特色包括線性設計、缺乏室內與室外間明確的界線及巨大的玻璃窗戶。

I. M. Pei's philosophy of design is also under the influence of Frank Lloyd Wright. One of his works of architecture in the Rocky Mountains in Colorado fits in with the natural environment seamlessly, echoing the feature mentioned in the reading. His design of the John F. Kennedy Presidential Library and Museum exhibits geometric forms and carries historic significance. Pei's most well-known building is the glass and steel pyramid at the Louvre Museum in Paris.

貝聿銘的設計理念也被法蘭克・洛伊・萊特影響。他設計的其中一棟建築位於科羅拉多州洛磯山脈，這棟建築和自然環境無縫地接合，呼應了閱讀篇章提到的特色。他對甘迺迪總統圖書館及紀念館的設計展現了幾何型式，並蘊含歷史意義。貝聿銘最知名的建築是位於巴黎羅浮宮博物館的玻璃及鋼鐵結構的金字塔。

高分範文解析

關鍵句 ①

Modern architecture is a comprehensive genre that includes architecture influenced by modernism, with identifiable traits such as functionality, simplicity, geometric shapes, and a harmonious relationship with surrounding environment.

解析

形容詞子句 that ... with surrounding environment. 是限定形容詞子句，關係代名詞 that 的先行詞是 genre；that 在此也是形容詞子句的主詞。副詞片語 with ... 強調形容詞子句提及的 architecture 的特色。

關鍵句 ②

One of his works of architecture in the Rocky Mountains in Colorado fits in with the natural environment seamlessly, echoing the feature mentioned in the reading.

解析

句尾的分詞片語 echoing... 是由形容詞子句 which echoes... 簡化而來。which 的先行詞是之前的完整子句 One of his works of archiectures...seamlessly。

閱讀短文中譯

請總結閱讀短文和課堂講述的重點，並著重於貝聿銘建築的特色。

現代建築是一個廣泛的稱呼，通常被套用在受到現代主義影響，於十九世紀末出現的建築，及那些有類似特色的二十世紀建築。跟之前的建築比起來，現代建築比較重視幾何型式、與地點的和諧關係和功能性超越裝飾性。

現代建築展現了某些特色，包括極簡設計、自然與建築融合及長方形和線性結構。在美國，最具代表性的是法蘭克・洛伊・萊特的建築，例如羅比屋和瀑布屋。法蘭克・洛伊・萊特被美國建築師學院稱為「歷史上最偉大的美國建築師」，因為他發展了「有機建築」這個美國原創的建築哲學，此哲學的意義在於建築應該融入自然環境當中。萊特的建築特色是直線元素。許多元素，例如橫梁、柱子、樓梯間和窗戶，都被利用來建構直線型空間。室內空間也延伸到戶外，形成另一個特色，即模糊了室內空間和戶外空間的界線。為了達到這種模糊界線，玻璃落地窗被使用。大片的玻璃不但引進自然光，也創造出莊嚴的視野。另一個示範玻璃窗能產生強大功能的經典例子是貝聿銘設計的玻璃金字塔，玻璃金字塔位於巴黎羅浮宮博物館。

1960 年代興起了一波波對現代建築的批評，自從 1960 年代，建築哲學的主流擁抱了後現代主義，現代主義就逐漸被取代了。

Now listen to a lecture in an art class regarding I. M. Pei, a renowned Chinese-American architect

現在請聽一篇關於知名華裔美籍建築師貝聿銘的藝術課堂講述。

(Professor) Ieoh Ming Pei, commonly known as I. M. Pei, is often referred to as the master of modern architecture. He was born in Guangzhou, China in 1917, and spent his childhood and adolescence in Hong Kong and Shanghai, where he was profoundly influenced by Hollywood movies and the style of colonial architecture.

貝聿銘，通常寫為 I. M. Pei 常被稱為現代建築大師。他於 1917 年在中國的廣州出生，童年及青少年時期在香港和上海度過，他在這兩個城市受到好萊塢電影和殖民式建築風格的深遠影響。

As Pei's secondary education in Shanghai drew near an end, he decided to enter an American university, a decision which he once admitted was made under the influence of Bing Crosby movies, in which college life in America seemed full of fun.

貝聿銘從在上海就讀高中快畢業時，他決定到美國念大學。他曾承認這個決定是受到賓・克洛斯比的電影影響，在那些電影裡，美國的大學生活似乎是充滿了歡樂。

Though he soon found out that the rigorous academic life differed drastically from the portrayal in the movies, he excelled in the architecture school of the Massachusetts Institute of Technology (MIT). Particularly, he was drawn to the school of modern architecture, featuring simplicity and the utilization of glass and steel materials, and influenced by architect Frank Lloyd Wright.

雖然他很快就發現嚴格的學術生活和電影的描繪相差甚多，他就讀於麻省理工學院的建築系時表現得非常優秀。他尤其被現代建築吸引，現代建築的特色是極簡風和運用玻璃及鋼鐵素材，他也被法蘭克・洛伊・萊特影響。

Throughout his career, Pei has designed numerous notable buildings. In 1961, he bcgan designing the Mesa Laboratory for the National Center for Atmospheric Research in Colorado.

在他的職業生涯中，貝聿銘設計了許多值得一提的建築。在 1961，他開始替位於科羅拉多州的國家人氣研究中心設計麥莎實驗室大樓。麥莎實驗室大樓展現了類似有機建築的哲學。

The Mesa Laboratory embodied his philosophy akin to Organic Architecture.The building rests harmoniously in the Rocky Mountains, as if sculpted out of rocks. Then, after President John F. Kennedy's assassination in 1963, Pei was chosen by Ms. Kennedy to design the John F. Kennedy Presidential Library and Museum, which includes a large square glass-enclosed courtyard with a triangular tower and a circular walkway.

這棟建築物和諧地和洛磯山脈並存,看起來像是直接從岩石雕鑿出來的。之後,在 1963 年甘迺迪總統被刺殺後,甘迺迪夫人選擇貝聿銘為甘迺迪總統圖書館及紀念館做設計。此圖書館及紀念館包含一大片被玻璃環繞的方形中庭、三角錐狀的高塔和圓形的走道。

Following some remarkable architectures in the U.S., such as Dallas City Hall, the Hancock Tower in Boston and the National Gallery East Building in Washington, D.C., Pei executed the most challenging project in his career in the 1980s, the renovation of the Louvre Museum in Paris.

在美國完成一些知名建築之後,例如達拉斯市政廳、波士頓的漢考克大廈和首府華盛頓的國家美術館東側大樓,貝聿銘於 1980 年代執行了職業生涯中最具挑戰性的案子,就是巴黎羅浮宮博物館的翻新工程。

His decision to build a huge glass and steel pyramid at the center of the courtyard initially ignited controversy, yet since its completion, the glass pyramid has become a famous landmark in Paris and Pei's most representative work.

他決定在羅浮宮中庭的中央建造一座巨型玻璃和鋼鐵金字塔,這個決定最初引起爭議,但是玻璃金字塔完成後,它成為巴黎知名的地標,也是貝聿銘最具代表性的作品。

西洋藝術類：
伍迪‧艾倫對戲劇的貢獻
Woody Allen's Contribution to Cinema

📖 INSTRUCTIONS

You have **20 minutes** to plan and write your response. Your response will be judged on the basis of the quality of your writing and on how well your response presents the points in the lecture and their relationships to the reading passage. Typically, an effective response will be 150 to 225 words.

Summarize the points made in the lecture you just heard, explaining how they cast doubt on points made in the reading.

Reading time: 3 minutes

Summarize the main points in the reading and the lecture

Woody Allen is undeniably one of the greatest American auteurs; his films carry a unique signature that makes his comic personae easily distinguishable from those in other Hollywood movies. In most of his films, the major personae exhibit neurotic disposition, and are frequently anxiety-ridden. Very often, those characters behave like schlemiels who undergo some sort of spiritual awakening or personal transformation through entanglements in relationships. With this comic portrayal, Allen presents philosophical issues in humorous ways, a theatrical scheme that he has developed since his early career as a stand-up comedian in Broadway in the 1960s.

Performing as stand-up comedian has exerted a substantial influence on his films, many of which are seemingly autobiographic, the most quintessential being *Annie Hall* (1977), which won 4 Academy Awards in 1978, including Best Actress for Diane Keaton, Best Script, Best Director and Best Picture, and was voted the funniest screenplay ever written by the Writers Guild of America in 2015. Although often categorized as a romantic comedy, *Annie Hall* actually breaks many traditions of this genre due to the experimental style, non-linear narrative akin to stream of consciousness, and the lack of a felicitous ending. As the story about the neurotic couple, Alvy and Annie, unfolds, viewers learn that it's not really about Alvy's lament on why the relationship ends, but on the perpetual loneliness of human existence.

Regarding the experimental nature of *Annie Hall*, Allen employed several unconventional visual techniques, such as split screens, animation, subtitles indicating the main characters' thoughts to contradict the onscreen dialogues, and the protagonist's direct address to the audience.

請聽與短文相關的課堂內容 ▶ *MP3 045*

Now listen to a lecture in a movie appreciation class regarding Woody Allen

（將聽到的重點，列在下列筆記欄內，並於練習後將記下的重點與高分範文的摘要重點作對照檢視是否記憶到關鍵重點。）

_____

_____

_____

_____

寫作實測

（在閱讀與播放音檔後，實際演練於 20 分鐘內完成整合題寫作，於電腦上打字完成 150-225 字數的英文。完成試題後請詳讀高分範文檢視與範文間的差異，強化應考實力）

_____

_____

_____

_____

整合能力強化① 訊息整合

比較「閱讀」和「聽力」講堂中內容的差異處，試著列出特點，比較特點後就能釐清主要差異或相似處，並著手開始寫作。

「閱讀」

* _____
* _____
* _____
* _____
* _____

「聽力」

* _____
* _____
* _____
* _____
* _____

整合訊息後，可以開始著手寫段落內容，寫完後可以與範文作對照。

* _____
* _____
* _____
* _____
* _____

整合能力強化② 聽力與口譯表達強化

① 知名的美國導演及喜劇演員，伍迪·艾倫，在 2015 年邁入杖朝之年，意思是他已經八十歲了。

_____

_____

ANS:

Renowned American director and comedian, Woody Allen, became an octogenarian in 2015, meaning he is in his 80s.

② 的確，這位備受讚賞的導演以這些電影成功地重返大螢幕，尤其是他不但因《午夜巴黎》得到奧斯卡金像獎最佳原創劇本獎及金球獎最佳劇本獎，而且《午夜巴黎》在北美洲的票房獲利是伍迪·艾倫所有的電影裡最高的。

_____

_____

ANS:

It is true that the highly-acclaimed director made a major comeback to the cinema with those movies, particularly with *Midnight in Paris*, which not only won him the Academy Award for Best Original Screenplay and the Golden Globe Award for Best Screenplay, but also attained the highest box office revenue in North America among all of Woody Allen's movies.

③ 若說伍迪・艾倫是天生的喜劇演員應該不為過。

_____

_____

ANS:

It is fair to say that Woody Allen is a natural born comedian.

④ 他和喜劇的關係早在 15 歲就開始了，他那時開始替在百老匯表演
的喜劇演員寫笑話，在 1955 年他 20 歲時，洛杉磯 NBC 電視台的
喜劇節目雇用他為全職作家，他為許多喜劇節目寫劇本。

_____

_____

ANS:

His involvement in comedy started very early at the age of 15
when he began writing jokes for comedians performing on
Broadway, and at age 20 in 1955, he was hired by The NBC
Comedy Hour on Los Angeles as a full-time writer for many
comedy shows.

⑤ 自此之後，他一直是位多產的作家，寫下眾多電視節目腳本，短
篇故事，喜劇小說和電影劇本。

_____

_____

ANS:

Since then, he has remained a prolific writer, having written
numerous TV show scripts, short stories, works of comic fiction,

and screenplays.

⑥ 在 1960 年代，他的才華延伸到單人脫口秀，他在曼哈頓的夜間俱樂部表演。

_____

_____

ANS:
He extended his caliber to stand-up comedy in the 1960s, performing as a stand-up comedian in nightclubs in Manhattan.

⑦ 在 1965 年，艾倫有了他個人的電視節目：伍迪‧艾倫秀，此時他成為全國知名的人物。

_____

_____

ANS:
Allen became well-known nationwide in 1965, when he had his own TV show, "The Woody Allen Show".

⑧ 神經質的角色之後成為他電影的特色。

_____

_____

ANS:
The neurotic persona later became a trademark in his movies.

高分範文搶先看 ▶ *MP3 046*

Both the reading and the lecture describe the features of the main characters in Woody Allen's movies. The reading emphasizes *Annie Hall*, and the listening elaborates on Allen's successful career.

閱讀篇章和課堂講述都描述了伍迪‧艾倫的電影裡主要角色的特點。閱讀篇章著重在《安妮‧霍爾》這部電影，而課堂講述詳細闡述艾倫成功的職業生涯。

According to the reading, Woody Allen's films carry a distinctive style that distinguishes his movies easily from the rest of the Hollywood movies. The major characters are usually angst-ridden people who behave clumsily and undergo changes in life when dealing with relationships. The comic elements are heavily influenced by Allen's early experiences of performing as a stand-up comedian. The film, *Annie Hall*, has received the most accolades among his abundant works. Regarded as a romantic comedy, Annie Hall was actually highly experimental because of its non-linear narrative, the lack of a happy ending, and various new filming techniques.

根據閱讀篇章，伍迪‧艾倫的電影有獨特的風格，使得他的電影容易和其他好萊塢電影區分開來。他的主要角色通常是感覺十分焦慮的人，而他們的行為笨拙，並在處理人際關係時經歷人生的變化。艾倫早期身為單人脫口秀表演者的經歷深遠地影響這種喜劇元素。在他豐富的作品中，《安妮‧霍爾》得到最多讚賞。《安妮‧霍爾》被視為一部浪漫喜劇，而事實上由於它非線性的敘述，缺少快樂的結局，及各式各樣新的拍片技巧，《安妮‧霍爾》是高度實驗性質的電影。

The lecture first raises the success of Allen's more recent films set in Europe, and then traces back to his budding career as a writer, stand-up comedian, and TV show host in the 1950s and 1960s. The protagonists in his comedies are characterized by a neurotic nature, and the prevalent theme is the absurdness of life expressed in satirical ways. Also, intellectuals and contemporary culture often become targets of his sarcasm.

課堂講述首先指出艾倫將場景設在歐洲的近期電影及其成功，接著回溯至他早期的職業， 他在 1950 和 1960 年代身為作家，單人脫口秀表演者及電視節目主持人。他的喜劇裡的主角有神經質特色，而常見的主題是以諷刺的方式表現出人生的荒謬。此外，知識份子和當代文化常成為他諷刺的對象。

高分範文解析

關鍵句 ①

The major characters are usually angst-ridden people who behave clumsily and undergo changes in life when dealing with relationships.

解析

此例句中的形容詞子句包含了一個分詞片語 when dealing with relationships，此分詞片語是由副詞子句 when they deal with relationships 簡化而來。代名詞 they 和關係代名詞 who 指的先行詞都是 angst-ridden people，兩個代名詞的指涉對象相同時，此副詞子句中的 they 才能省略，並將副詞子句簡化成分詞片語。

關鍵句 ②

Regarded as a romantic comedy, *Annie Hall* was actually highly experimental because of its non-linear narrative, the lack of a happy ending, and various new techniques.

解析

分詞片語在句首一定是修飾主詞，因為主詞是電影名稱 *Annie Hall*，所以分詞片語以過去分詞 regarded 表達被動，意思是：被視為。

請總結閱讀短文和課堂講述的重點。

伍迪・艾倫無疑是美國導演中，個人風格強烈的最偉大導演之一。他的電影有獨特風格，使他的喜劇角色能輕易地和其他好萊塢喜劇角色區分。在他的大部份電影裡，主要角色展現神經質的特色，而且常常感到焦慮。那些角色常表現笨拙，並透過人際關係的牽扯，經歷某種靈性覺醒或個人蛻變。艾倫運用這種喜劇手法的描繪，以幽默的方式提出哲學議題，自從他的早期職業，即 1960 年代在百老匯表演單人脫口秀時，他就已經發展這種戲劇手法。

單人脫口秀表演對他的電影有深厚的影響，他的許多電影似乎都具備自傳性質，最具代表性的是《安妮・霍爾》（1977），這部電影在 1978 年得到四座奧斯卡金像獎，包括黛安・基頓贏得最佳女主角獎，最佳劇本獎，最佳導演獎及最佳影片獎，並在 2015 年由美國作家協會投票選為史上最有趣的劇本。雖然《安妮・霍爾》常被歸類在浪漫喜劇，由於這部電影的實驗風格，類似意識流的非線性敘述，及缺乏幸福結局，它其實打破許多這個類型的傳統。隨著電影裡阿飛和安妮這對神經質情侶的故事展開，觀眾漸漸知道電影內容並不是真的關於阿飛在悼念為何這段感情結束，而是關於人類生存的持續寂寞狀態。

關於《安妮・霍爾》的實驗性質，艾倫運用了幾個非典型的視覺技巧，例如分割螢幕畫面、動畫、字幕顯示的是主要角色的想法，和他們對話的內容是相反的，及主角直接向觀眾說話。

聽力原文和中譯

Now listen to a lecture in a movie appreciation class regarding Woody Allen

現在請聽一篇關於伍迪・艾倫的電影賞析課堂講述。

(Professor) Renowned American director and comedian, Woody Allen, became an octogenarian in 2015, meaning he is in his 80s. The younger generation of audiences might not be so familiar with his early career, although many have acquainted themselves with Woody Allen's more recent movies set in major European cities, such as *Match Point*, set in London and released in 2005, *Midnight in Paris*, released in 2011, and *To Rome with Love*, released in 2012. It is true that the highly-acclaimed director made a major comeback in the cinema with those movies, particularly with *Midnight in Paris*, which not only won him the Academy Award for Best Original Screenplay and the Golden Globe Award for Best Screenplay, but also attained the highest box office revenue in North America among all of Woody Allen's movies.

知名的美國導演及喜劇演員，伍迪・艾倫，在 2015 年邁入杖朝之年，意思是他已經八十歲了。較年輕的觀眾可能對他早期的職涯不是很熟悉，雖然很多人熟悉伍迪・艾倫近年來將場景設在歐洲主要城市的電影，例如場景在倫敦並於 2005 年上映的《愛情決勝點》、2011 年上映的《午夜巴黎》及 2012 年上映的《愛上羅馬》。的確，這位備受讚賞的導演以這些電影成功地重返大螢幕，尤其是他不但因《午夜巴黎》得到奧斯卡金像獎最佳原創劇本獎及金球獎最佳劇本獎，而且《午夜巴黎》在北美洲的票房獲利是伍迪・艾倫所有的電影裡最高的。

It is fair to say that Woody Allen is a natural born comedian. His involvement in comedy started very early at the age of 15 when he began writing jokes for comedians performing on Broadway, and at age 20 in 1955, he was hired by The NBC Comedy Hour on Los Angeles as a full-time writer for many comedy shows. Since then, he has remained a prolific writer, having written numerous TV show scripts, short stories, works of comic fiction, and screenplays. He extended his caliber to stand-up comedy in the 1960s, performing as a stand-up comedian in nightclubs in Manhattan. Allen became well-known nationwide in 1965, when he had his own TV show, "The Woody Allen Show".

若說伍迪・艾倫是天生的喜劇演員應該不為過。他和喜劇的關係早在 15 歲就開始了，他那時開始替在百老匯表演的喜劇演員寫笑話，在 1955 年他 20 歲時，洛杉磯 NBC 電視台的喜劇節目雇用他為全職作家，他為許多喜劇節目寫劇本。自此之後，他一直是位多產的作家，寫下眾多電視節目腳本，短篇故事，喜劇小說和電影劇本。在 1960 年代，他的才華延伸到單人脫口秀，他在曼哈頓的夜間俱樂部表演。在 1965 年，艾倫有了他個人的電視節目：伍迪・艾倫秀，此時他成為全國知名的人物。

The common theme of Allen's films, that is, the satirical reflection of the absurdity of life, can be traced to his early works. His jokes were based on daily incidents that everyone could relate to, but were performed with very serious and neurotic expressions. The neurotic persona later became a trademark in his movies. In his stand-up comedies, he often satirized intellectuals and turned monologues into ironic remarks on contemporary cultural phenomena.

艾倫的電影的普遍主題，即諷刺地反映人生的荒謬之處，可以追溯至他早期的作品。他的笑話是依據每個人都能感同身受的日常事件，但是以非常嚴肅和神經質的表達方式演出。神經質的角色之後成為他電影的特色。在他的單人脫口秀，他經常諷刺知識份子，並將獨白轉化成對當代文化現象的嘲諷批評。

UNIT 10

科學類：
玩耍對動物的重要性
The Importance of Play for Animals

📖 INSTRUCTIONS

You have **20 minutes** to plan and write your response. Your response will be judged on the basis of the quality of your writing and on how well your response presents the points in the lecture and their relationships to the reading passage. Typically, an effective response will be 150 to 225 words.

Summarize the points made in the lecture you just heard, explaining how they cast doubt on points made in the reading.

Reading time: 3 minutes

Summarize the main points in the reading and the lecture

People who have puppies or kittens know very well that they spend significant amount of time on playing. How do we distinguish nonhuman animals' play from actual fighting? How do animals communicate to their playmates so that their partners know their intent is to play?

To answer the above questions, the meaning of play should be clarified first. Basically, play refers to behaviors of mimicking actual hunting, fighting and mating carried out by adults. One way to distinguish play from the aforementioned adult behaviors is to observe that when young animals engage in play, their mimicking behaviors do not exhibit fixed sequences; in other words, they are performed and combined randomly. Another sign of play is that these behaviors are less intense compared with adult behaviors.

As for communicating to their partners to initiate play, animals use facial expressions and gestures to send out signals. Take dogs for example, dogs are in the mood for play when their facial expressions are placid and mild, with their mouths slightly open, which many dog owners describe as a "smile". Canines, including dogs, wolves, and coyotes, all employ the gesture of "play bow" to signal to their playmates. It is worth noting that "play bow" is exclusive to canines. Their front limbs stand firm, heads duck quickly, and hind limbs kick up. Besides facial expressions and gestures, dogs even signal verbally. The verbal signal is their panting noise in play, which has a different frequency from the frequency of panting when they are not playing.

請聽與短文相關的課堂內容 ▶ *MP3 047*

Now listen to a lecture in a biology class regarding animal play

（將聽到的重點，列在下列筆記欄內，並於練習後將記下的重點與高分範文的摘要重點作對照檢視是否記憶到關鍵重點。）

_____

_____

_____

_____

_____

寫作實測

（在閱讀與播放音檔後，實際演練於 20 分鐘內完成整合題寫作，於電腦上打字完成 150-225 字數的英文。完成試題後請詳讀高分範文檢視與範文間的差異，強化應考實力）

_____

_____

_____

_____

_____

整合能力強化① 訊息整合

比較「閱讀」和「聽力」講堂中內容的差異處，試著列出特點，比較特點後就能釐清主要差異或相似處，並著手開始寫作。

「閱讀」

* _____
* _____
* _____
* _____
* _____

「聽力」

* _____
* _____
* _____
* _____
* _____

整合訊息後，可以開始著手寫段落內容，寫完後可以與範文作對照。

* _____
* _____
* _____
* _____
* _____

整合能力強化② 聽力與口譯表達強化

① 第三個類型是物體玩耍，常常是獨自進行並和捕食玩耍合併，雖然不見得總是這樣。

_____

_____

ANS:

The third type is object play, which is often played solitarily and combined with predatory play, though not always.

② 例如，由於靈長類的肢體靈巧，他們玩各種物體的方式和人類小孩玩耍的方式是類似的。

_____

_____

ANS:

For instance, primates, due to their adroitness, play with various objects in a similar way as human children do.

③ 在進行物體玩耍時，靈長類已經被證實會展現想像力。

_____

_____

ANS:

Primates have been proven to demonstrate their imagination in object play.

Part 1
獨立篇

Part 2
整合篇

④ 在一個研究中，一隻曾受過手語訓練的黑猩猩將一個皮包放在腳上，並比出「鞋子」的手語。

_____

_____

ANS:

In research, a chimpanzee having been trained to use sign language placed a purse on his foot, and gave the sign for "shoe".

⑤ 第四個類型是社交玩耍，讓動物建立友誼，學習合作，並模仿成年競爭性的行為，但不會展現暴力。

_____

_____

ANS:

The fourth type is social play, which allows animals to form friendship, learn cooperation, and mimic adult competitive behaviors without acting violent.

⑥ 關於玩耍的益處，我想專注在對頭腦的影響，既然你們已經知道玩耍對肌肉發展和協調是重要的。

_____

_____

ANS:

Regarding the benefits of play, I would like to focus on the effects on the brain, since you already know that play is crucial in developing muscle and coordination.

⑦ 情緒上，玩耍就是讓動物覺得放鬆，比較沒壓力。

_____

_____

ANS:
Emotionally, play just makes animals feel relaxed and less stressed.

⑧ 當玩耍時，他們碰觸彼此最多，而碰觸會刺激腦內一種稱為鴉片類物質的化學物質，這化學物質會產生放鬆的感覺。

_____

_____

ANS:
They touch one another the most when playing, and touching stimulates a chemical in the brain called opiate, which generates a soothing feeling.

⑨ 此外，玩耍加強腦內神經細胞的連結。

_____

_____

ANS:
Moreover, play enhances neuron connections in the brain.

高分範文搶先看 ▶ MP3 048

Both the reading and the lecture concern the theme of animal play. The reading gives the definition of play and describes how animals communicate to one another about their intent to play, and the lecture provides more details regarding the types and benefits of play.

閱讀篇章和課堂講述都是關於動物玩耍的主題。閱讀篇章給了玩耍的定義及描述動物如何彼此溝通關於他們想玩的意圖，而課堂講述提供更多關於玩耍的類型和益處等細節。

The reading defines animal play as mimicking a variety of adult behaviors. Unlike adult behaviors, young animals' play does not follow any order, and is less violent. Facial expressions and gestures are utilized to communicate to partners to begin playing. Canines are used as an example to illustrate signals of communication. Dogs have a smile-like expression, and all canines display "play bow". A different frequency of panting is also an indicator.

閱讀篇章將動物玩耍定義為模仿各式各樣成年行為。不像成年行為，年輕動物的玩耍不按照任何順序，而且比較不暴力。表情和肢體動作被用來向玩伴溝通以開始玩耍。以犬類為例，描繪溝通的訊號。狗有一種類似微笑的表情，而所有犬類都展現「玩耍敬禮」。喘息的不同頻率也是一個跡象。

The lecture first lists four kinds of play: locomotor , predatory, object, and social play. Locomotor play enhances muscular and coordinative movements. Predatory play imitates hunting. Object play, for primates particularly, is similar to human children's play of objects. Social play builds animals' socializing skills. Finally, the benefit of how play simulates the brain by reinforcing a certain chemical and neuron connections is explained.

課堂講述先列舉四種玩耍：運動、捕食、物體和社交玩耍。運動玩耍加強肌肉和協調動作。捕食玩耍模仿打獵。物體玩耍，尤其對靈長類而言，類似人類小孩玩物體的行為。社交玩耍建立動物的社交技巧。最後解釋玩耍如何藉由增強某種化學物質及神經細胞連結，以刺激頭腦的這個益處。

高分範文解析

關鍵句 ①

Facial expressions and gestures are utilized to communicate to partners to begin playing.

解析

句型的豐富度是評分重點之一，應輪流使用主動和被動語態的句型。此句是被動語態，動詞 utilize 比 use 語氣更正式。被動語態的主要動詞是 be 動詞搭配過去分詞 is explained。

關鍵句 ②

Finally, the benefit of how play stimulates the brain by reinforcing a certain chemical and neuron connections is explained.

解析

此句是被動語態句型，介系詞 of 之後的受詞是由 how 引導的名詞子句。reinforcing 是動名詞，以搭配介系詞 by。

閱讀短文中譯

請總結閱讀短文和課堂講述的重點。

有養幼犬或幼貓的人一定知道他們花很多時間玩耍。我們要如何區分非人類的動物是在玩耍，還是實際在打架呢？動物是如何跟玩伴們溝通，讓玩伴知道他們想玩耍的意圖呢？

要回答以上的問題，玩耍的定義應該先被釐清。基本上，玩耍指的是模仿成年動物實際打獵、打鬥和交配的行為。一個區分上述成年行為和玩耍的方式是去觀察當幼年動物玩耍，他們的模仿行為沒有固定的順序；也就是說他們是任意地表現和結合這些行為。另一個跡象是這些行為比起成年行為沒那麼激烈。

關於如何和玩伴們溝通以開始玩耍，動物利用表情和肢體動作傳送訊息。以狗為例，當他們的表情冷靜溫和，嘴巴稍微張開，就是準備好玩耍，許多狗主人將這個表情描述為「微笑」。犬類，包括狗、狼和郊狼，都使用「玩耍敬禮」這個肢體動作傳送訊息給玩伴。值得注意的是「玩耍敬禮」是犬類獨特有的行為。他們的前腿穩穩地站著，縮頸躬身且快速地點頭，後腿向上踢。除了表情和肢體動作，狗甚至會傳送口語訊號。口語訊號指的是他們玩耍時發出的喘氣聲，這種喘氣聲的頻率和不是在玩耍時的喘氣聲的頻率是不同的。

 聽力原文和中譯

Now listen to a lecture in a biology class regarding animal play

現在請聽一篇關於動物玩耍的生物學課堂講述。

(Professor)In today's lecture, we are going to cover more details concerning the play of young animals. In particular, how many types of animal play have biologists discerned so far? And what are the benefits? The first type is locomotor play. As the word locomotor implies, this type of play strengthens muscle and physical coordination. The second type is predatory play, in which animals stalk and swoop upon playmates to mimic hunting behaviors. Even birds, such as falcons, crows, and swallows, engage in predatory play; they drop tiny objects from above and descend rapidly to catch those objects.

今天的講課，我們將涵蓋更多關於年輕動物玩耍的細節。尤其，科學家至目前分析了多少種動物玩耍的類型？玩耍的好處有哪些？第一種類型是運動玩耍。就像運動這個字暗示的，這個類型加強肌肉和身體協調能力。第二種類型是捕食玩耍，玩耍當中動物會尾隨並突然襲擊玩伴，這是在模仿打獵行為。甚至鳥類，例如獵鷹、烏鴉和燕子，也會進行捕食玩耍。他們會從高處丟下小型物體，然後快速下降去抓那些物體。

345

The third type is object play, which is often played solitarily and combined with predatory play, though not always. For instance, primates, due to their adroitness, play with various objects in a similar way as human children do. Primates have been proven to demonstrate their imagination in object play. In research, a chimpanzee having been trained to use sign language placed a purse on his foot, and gave the sign for "shoe". The fourth type is social play, which allows animals to form friendship, learn cooperation, and mimic adult competitive behaviors without acting violent.

第三個類型是物體玩耍，常常是獨自進行並和捕食玩耍合併，雖然不見得總是這樣。例如，由於靈長類的肢體靈巧，他們玩各種物體的方式和人類小孩玩耍的方式是類似的。在進行物體玩耍時，靈長類已經被證實會展現想像力。在一個研究中，一隻曾受過手語訓練的黑猩猩將一個皮包放在腳上，並比出「鞋子」的手語。第四個類型是社交玩耍，讓動物建立友誼，學習合作，並模仿成年競爭性的行為，但不會展現暴力。

Regarding the benefits of play, I would like to focus on the effects on the brain, since you already know that play is crucial in developing muscle and coordination. Emotionally, play just makes animals feel relaxed and less stressed. They touch one another the most when playing, and touching stimulates a chemical in the brain called opiate, which generates a soothing feeling. Moreover, play enhances neuron connections in the brain. The stronger neuron connections are, the more efficiently brains function, which makes animals more intelligent. For mammals, play even helps remove superfluous brain cells, and prepares their brains to function more efficiently during adulthood. To sum up, there are at least four areas that play exerts positive effects on: physical, social, emotional, and intelligent areas.

關於玩耍的益處，我想專注在對頭腦的影響，既然你們已經知道玩耍對肌肉發展和協調是重要的。情緒上，玩耍就是讓動物覺得放鬆，比較沒壓力。當玩耍時，他們碰觸彼此最多，而碰觸會刺激腦內一種稱為鴉片類物質的化學物質，這化學物質會產生放鬆的感覺。此外，玩耍加強腦內神經細胞的連結。神經細胞連結越強，頭腦運作地更有效率，這讓動物更聰明。對哺乳類而言，玩耍甚至會幫助清除多餘的腦細胞，讓他們的頭腦為成年時期更高效率的運作做準備。總之，玩耍至少在四個方面發揮正面效應：生理、社交、情緒和智能方面。

新托福寫作引用和出處

頁數	參考書籍	引述句子
作者序	*The Third Door*	"Bill Gates and Mark Zuckerberg didn't drop out the way you think they did. Do some research." (Alex, 2018, p.133)
作者序	*The Third Door*	"Gates didn't impulsively drop out of college either. He took just one semester off during junior year to work full-time on Microsoft." (Alex, 2018, p.134)
p.33	*The Promise of A Pencil: How ordinary Person Can Create Extraordinary Change*	"Brauns are different". (Adam, 2014, p.6)
p.33	*The Promise of A Pencil: How ordinary Person Can Create Extraordinary Change*	"we developed an inherent drive to live into the ideals they had defined us". (Adam, 2014, p.7)
p.58	*Desperate Housewives* (Season one)	"I have four kids under the age of six. I absolutely have anger management issues."
p.58	*Desperate Housewives* (Season three)	"If I threw a little slower, then I would be playing bowing."
p.106	*How Luck Happens*	"You and your best friends already know most of the same people - you have overlapping social circles". (Janice and Barnaby, 2018, p.69)
p.117	*Getting There*	"Many students are so focused on getting the right grades so that they can get into the right school that it barely gives them the chance to do something zany". (Gillian, 2015, p.175)

頁數	參考書籍	引述句子
p.141	*Getting There*	"When you are much more interested in what you're doing than going out for a drink with friends, you've found your bliss". (Gillian, 2015, p.43)
p.142	*What I Wish I Knew When I was 20*	"the goal should be a career in which you can't believe people actually pay you to do your job." (Tina, 2009, p.100-101)
p.152	*How Will You Measure Your Life*	"parents, often with their heart in the right place, project their own hopes and dreams onto their children" (Clayton, 2012, p.132)
p.152	*How Will You Measure Your Life*	"when these other intentions start creeping in, and parents seem to be charting their children around to an endless array of activities in which the kids are not truly engaged…". (Clayton, 2012, p.132)
p.165	*Peak, Secrets from the New Science of Expertise*	"In almost every one of the five dozen studies included in the review, doctors' performance grew worse over time or stayed about the same. " (Anders and Robert, 2017, p.133)
p.165	*Peak, Secrets from the New Science of Expertise*	"The older doctors knew less and did worse in terms of providing appropriate care than doctors with far fewer years of experience." (Anders and Robert, 2017, p.133)
p.166	*Peak, Secrets from the New Science of Expertise*	"if continuing education does not keep doctors effectively updated, then the older they get, the less current their skill will be". (Anders and Robert, 2017, p.133)

英文文法・生活英語

用最瑣碎的時間 建立學習自信
輕鬆打下英語學習基礎！
■用心智圖概念，圖「解」複雜又難吸收的文法觀念
■30天學習進度規劃，不出國也能變身ABC
■規劃三大階段學習法，拋開制式學習，更有成效！

英文文法超圖解　　　定價 NT$ 369
ISBN：9789869528825
書系編號：文法/生活英語系列 005
書籍規格：386頁/18K/普通級/雙色印刷/平裝

說文解詩學文法　「戀」習英語寫作
精選「經典」英美情詩附中英對照，引用的詩句對應文法
概念，並且提供英語寫作範文與中譯，幫助讀者掌握寫作
起、承、轉、合的訣竅，優雅閱讀同時提升寫作功力！

學文法，戀習英語寫作　　　定價 NT$ 369
ISBN：9789869285544
書系編號：Learn Smart 062
書籍規格：304頁/18K/普通級/雙色印刷/平裝

結合英、法語字彙　享受甜點＋下午茶
語言學習的多重樂趣
精選與甜點、下午茶有關的英文字彙，皆附例句以及法語
字彙，且由專業錄音老師錄製英文單字、例句和法語單字
，學會最正統的發音！特別企劃【魔法廚房】由前輩親授
製作甜點的秘訣與心得，提供調整、創新口味的建議，幫
助店家製作出口感更符合東方人的點心，提高自家產品的
接受度與流行度！

Bon Appetit 甜點物語：英法語字彙 (附MP3)定價 NT$ 360
ISBN：9789869285582
書系編號：Learn Smart　065
書籍規格：288頁/18K/普通級/雙色印刷/平裝附光碟

─ 親子英語 ─

在家就能輕鬆打造親子英語教室
小學生必備的基礎學科通通有

將家庭教育、英語學習和學校課程巧妙融入本書，內容涵蓋天文、地理、生物、科學、人文藝術，主題引導學習，讓小朋友聽得懂，讀得下去。是兼具實用和趣味的親子英語共讀書。

我的第一本萬用親子英語 (附MP3)
定價 NT$ 399
ISBN：9789869528894
書系編號：文法/生活英語系列 006
書籍規格：224頁/18K/普通級/全彩印刷/平裝附光碟

結合自然發音與KK音標的圖解發音書
解決學習發音的困擾

單元特色：
◎50個音標+6組字尾聯音：迅速辨認音標與發音規則
◎8組繞口令：透過反覆練習繞口令，矯正英文發音，加強口齒伶俐度
◎老師獨門音節劃分法：劃分音節，輕鬆讀出英文長字

圖解英文發音二重奏：自然發音、KK音標 (附MP3)
定價 NT$ 369
ISBN：9789869191586
書系編號：Learn Smart 055
書籍規格：288頁/18K/普通級/雙色印刷/平裝附光碟

運用思考力、創意力和英語力
編織屬於自己的童話故事

加入許多科技元素、高科技產品於故事情節中，融入許多道地語彙及美式幽默，更將童話故事中人物善惡對調，kuso的情節激起許多風波和笑點，引領讀者品味不同的故事。學習另一種活潑、新穎的說法，讓你的口語英文更自然。

童話奇緣：Follow Kuso英語童話，來一場穿越時空之旅 (附MP3)
定價 NT$ 380
ISBN：9789869191555
書系編號：Learn Smart 052
書籍規格：332頁/18K/普通級/雙色印刷/平裝附光碟

國家圖書館出版品預行編目(CIP)資料

新托福100⁺iBT寫作/韋爾、倍斯特編輯部著.
-- 初版.-- 新北市：倍斯特出版事業有限公司
, 民111.06　面；　公分. --（考用英語系列
; 039）　ISBN 978-626-95434-7-2(平裝)
1.CST: 托福考試　2.CST: 寫作法

805.1894　　　　　　　　　　111007514

考用英語系列　039

新托福100⁺iBT寫作（附QR code音檔）

初版二刷　　2022年6月
定　　價　　新台幣460元

作　　者　　韋爾、倍斯特編輯部
出　　版　　倍斯特出版事業有限公司
發 行 人　　周瑞德
電　　話　　886-2-8245-6905
傳　　真　　886-2-2245-6398
地　　址　　23558 新北市中和區立業路83巷7號4樓
E - m a i l　　best.books.service@gmail.com
官　　網　　www.bestbookstw.com
總 編 輯　　齊心瑀
特約編輯　　James Chiao
封面構成　　高鍾琪
內頁構成　　菩薩蠻數位文化有限公司
印　　製　　大亞彩色印刷製版股份有限公司

港澳地區總經銷　　泛華發行代理有限公司
地　　址　　香港新界將軍澳工業邨駿昌街7號2樓
電　　話　　852-2798-2323
傳　　真　　852-3181-3973